Easy With You

Also by Kristen Proby

The Boudreaux Series:

Easy Love

The With Me In Seattle Series:

Come Away With Me
Under the Mistletoe With Me
Fight With Me
Play With Me
Rock With Me

Safe With Me
Tied With Me
Breathe With Me
Forever With Me

The Love Under the Big Sky Series (published by Pocket Books):

Loving Cara

Seducing Lauren
Falling for Jillian
Baby, It's Cold Outside: An Anthology with Jennifer Probst,
Emma Chase, Kristen Proby, Melody Anne and Kate Meader

Easy With You

A With Me In Seattle Novella

By Kristen Proby

1001 Dark Nights

EVIL EYE
CONCEPTS

Easy With You
A With Me In Seattle Novella
By Kristen Proby

1001 Dark Nights
Copyright 2015 Kristen Proby
Print ISBN: 978-1-940887-81-4

Foreword: Copyright 2014 M. J. Rose
Published by Evil Eye Concepts, Incorporated

Sign up for the 1001 Dark Nights Newsletter
and be entered to win a Tiffany Key necklace.

There's a contest every month!

Go to www.1001DarkNights.com to subscribe.

As a bonus, all newsletter subscribers will receive a free
1001 Dark Nights story
The First Night
by Lexi Blake & M.J. Rose

One Thousand and One Dark Nights

Once upon a time, in the future…

*I was a student fascinated with stories and learning.
I studied philosophy, poetry, history, the occult, and
the art and science of love and magic. I had a vast
library at my father's home and collected thousands
of volumes of fantastic tales.*

*I learned all about ancient races and bygone
times. About myths and legends and dreams of all
people through the millennium. And the more I read
the stronger my imagination grew until I discovered
that I was able to travel into the stories... to actually
become part of them.*

*I wish I could say that I listened to my teacher
and respected my gift, as I ought to have. If I had, I
would not be telling you this tale now.
But I was foolhardy and confused, showing off
with bravery.*

*One afternoon, curious about the myth of the
Arabian Nights, I traveled back to ancient Persia to
see for myself if it was true that every day Shahryar
(Persian: شهريار, "king") married a new virgin, and then*

sent yesterday's wife to be beheaded. It was written and I had read, that by the time he met Scheherazade, the vizier's daughter, he'd killed one thousand women.

Something went wrong with my efforts. I arrived in the midst of the story and somehow exchanged places with Scheherazade — a phenomena that had never occurred before and that still to this day, I cannot explain.

Now I am trapped in that ancient past. I have taken on Scheherazade's life and the only way I can protect myself and stay alive is to do what she did to protect herself and stay alive.

Every night the King calls for me and listens as I spin tales. And when the evening ends and dawn breaks, I stop at a point that leaves him breathless and yearning for more. And so the King spares my life for one more day, so that he might hear the rest of my dark tale.

As soon as I finish a story... I begin a new one... like the one that you, dear reader, have before you now.

Prologue

~Asher~

"You should consider moving here," Mike says and takes a pull of the long-neck bottle of his beer, then shifts his gaze from the baseball game on the screen above the bar to me. We're in the heart of the French Quarter in New Orleans, at some bar on Bourbon Street, having a few beers after a long day of work.

I shake my head. I've heard this line from my brother at least a dozen times since he and his wife moved here from New York last year.

"I'm happy in Seattle. Casey's happy in Seattle."

"Casey will be happy wherever you're happy," Mike replies. "Don't you want to be close to family?"

"I'd be kicking your ass all the time," I reply. "You'd be begging me to leave in a week."

"You could try, little brother," Mike says with a smirk. "The force could use you."

I shrug a shoulder and drink my beer. I like working for the Seattle force. I have a dependable partner. Casey does well in school. But there's no family for us there, and I admit it's hard when my babysitter bails on me.

Being a single father fucking sucks.

"I'll think about it."

Mike nods and checks his phone when it lights up with a text. A group of girls behind us are laughing loudly, clearly having a good time. I wonder if it's a bachelorette party.

"Franny's wondering when I'm coming home," Mike says with a smile. "I'm getting laid, buddy."

I laugh and shake my head as I take a drink of my beer. "Good for you, buddy."

"Yes, she is good for me," he agrees.

"Ten years and two kids later and you still get that shit-eating grin on your face." I smile, happy for my brother.

"Of course, I love her." He shoves his phone in his pocket, swallows the last of his beer, and claps his hand on my shoulder as he climbs off his stool. "I'm out. See you tomorrow."

"Goodnight."

Suddenly, the sexy redhead from the group behind me is standing next to me at the bar, blinking her glassy green eyes. "Hi there."

"Hi."

"Having a good time?" I ask with a grin.

"Yes." She blinks some more, and then her eyes widen in recognition. "I know you!"

"You do?" I'm quite sure I'd know if I'd met this woman.

"Yes! You were on the plane with Lila yesterday. Asher?"

"That's right." I take her offered hand and shake it, immediately remembering the gorgeous woman I caught in my lap on the plane. "Is Lila with you this evening?"

And if she is, how in the ever-loving hell did I miss her?

"Yep. She's my BFF. We drink together. One time in college we made out, but it was no biggie."

"Okay." I laugh, wishing I'd been there to see that.

"You didn't ask for her number." She scowls and pokes her finger into my chest. I look down at it, then glance up at her with a raised brow.

"You just assaulted an officer."

"I did?" She swallows hard.

"Yes. I might have to arrest you."

"With handcuffs?" She smiles gleefully, clearly excited at the thought.

"Would you like me to arrest you with handcuffs?"

"Hell to the yes!"

"Kate?" There's suddenly a very tall, very irritated man standing behind the fiery redhead, staring daggers into me. I can't help but laugh.

"I'm talking to the hot Asher," she says, not turning to look at him. "I assaulted him, and he's a cop, and he's going to put me in handcuffs."

"No, I don't believe he will."

I laugh again. "There's nothing going on here, man."

"Come see Lila!" Kate takes my hand, pulling me from my stool to the table behind us. Most of the women have cleared out, leaving just a few, including the sexy as fuck woman I met on the plane yesterday. "Where did everyone go?"

"Declan took them home," Lila replies, and her hand stops midway between the table and her lips, holding her drink. Her violet eyes widen when she sees me. "Hi."

"We meet again." I sit next to her, my fingers itching to plunge in her dark hair and brush it over her shoulder. "How are you, Lila?"

"Fine." She clears her throat and smiles at me. "I didn't think I'd ever see you again."

"A happy coincidence," I reply softly. "You look beautiful."

And she does. Her eyes are a bit glassy from the alcohol, her cheeks just a little flushed. Her hair is straight and falls down her back and over her slim shoulders. Before I can ask her questions about her trip here, or anything about her, we are soon pulled into the conversation with the others at the table. But when Kate asks Lila if she's ready to go, I'm shocked when

Lila responds with, "I'm gonna have Asher take me home."

"Atta girl!" Kate high-fives Lila, making me chuckle, then turns her sights on me. "And listen up, buddy. If you hurt her, I don't care if you really are a cop, I'll make your life hell. Okay?"

"Okay." I nod soberly, glad that Lila has such fiercely loyal friends in her life.

And I barely know her.

"I hope that's okay," Lila says and turns to me with an embarrassed smile.

"More than okay." I can't help it. I have to touch her. I tuck her hair behind her ear with my fingertip and then drag it down her jawline. "But I don't think I want to take you home and end the evening."

"I don't either," she whispers, her eyes fixed on my lips. She licks hers, and just like that I'm hard as fuck. "And that's very unlike me."

"Oh?"

She nods soberly. "I don't do this sort of thing."

"What sort of thing would this be?" I lean into her, enjoying the smell of her, the way her eyes dilate as I get closer.

"Pick up strange men."

"Well, I'm not exactly a stranger. I mean, you've already been in my lap, after all." I smile down at her, enjoying the way her cheeks redden at the memory of her falling into my lap on the plane yesterday.

"You didn't seem to mind."

Oh, trust me, sweetheart, I didn't mind at all.

"Would it be okay if I took you back to my hotel? It's a couple blocks away."

"You're bold," she says with a flirty grin. "And I think I'd like that."

I stand, take her hand, and pull her to her feet, then lead her out of the bar and onto the busy street. She's in mile-high heels, which are going to look fantastic over my shoulders, but are not appropriate for walking around New Orleans.

When she stumbles about a block away from the hotel, I simply lift her in my arms and carry her the rest of the way.

"You're strong." She loops her arms around my neck and presses her nose to my cheek. "And you smell good."

"And if you keep running your fingers through my hair like that, I'm going to fuck you right here, against the side of the hotel," I inform her, my voice completely calm but clear. She simply laughs and kisses my cheek.

"I'm sure we wouldn't be the first people to fuck against the side of this hotel. This is New Orleans." She smirks as I set her on her feet by the elevator.

"True enough."

When the elevators arrive, she saunters in, leans her back against the far wall, and crooks her finger at me, inviting me to join her.

And who the fuck can resist that?

"You're sexy," I murmur and kiss her forehead. She plants her hands on my sides, gripping my shirt in her small fists. God, she's the sexiest thing I've seen in a very long time, and not only is coming here with me out of character for her, it's completely new to me too.

I don't do one-night stands.

Fuck, I don't date much.

Having a young daughter will do that to you.

"So are you."

The elevator arrives on my floor. I escort her calmly to my room, open the door and motion for her to lead me inside. And as soon as the door closes, I grip her shoulders in my hands and spin her, pinning her back against the door with my body. I plant my hands on either side of her head and lean in, not kissing her. Not yet. Her eyes are wide, staring at my lips again, pulse thrumming, panting.

She's so fucking sexy I can hardly breathe.

"I want to fuck you, Lila."

"Oh good." She swallows. "We're on the same page. I want to fuck you too."

"No, sweetheart." I grin and lower my face beside hers. I'm not touching her, but I can feel her. Our skin is *almost* touching, and I know I'm making her crazy.

I'm making *me* fucking crazy.

"*I'm* going to fuck *you*." I drag my nose along her earlobe and grin when she shivers. "But first, I think we could use something to cool us off."

"Cool us off?" she whispers.

Without touching her, I back away, take her hand and walk to the small wet bar in my room, open a bottle of Patrón that one of the guys at the precinct gave me, slice a lime and reach for the salt shaker sitting on my room service tray from lunch, relieved that I forgot to set it in the hallway on my way out this afternoon.

"Have you ever done body shots?" I ask her. She's watching me closely, her hip leaning against the counter, arms crossed over her chest.

"No." She shakes her head and bites her lip.

"Wanna do them with me?"

"Yes."

"I'll go first." I pull her to me, her stomach against my pelvis, and push her hair over her shoulder. "Tip your head back, please."

She complies, and I lick a short path down the side of her neck, making her breath catch. God, she's so damn responsive. I shake a little salt on the wet spot, then lick it clean, take the shot, and suck on the lime.

Her eyes never leave me. I love that she's not shy.

"My turn," she says as she unbuttons my shirt and pushes it aside. She stands on her tiptoes and licks right under my collarbone, as that's as high as she can reach, then repeats the process, making me even harder at the feel of her sweet lips and tongue on my skin.

When she's done, I turn her around and lick down the back of her neck, her shoulder, and pull the strap of her dress down her arm, drag my fingertips over her skin, making her shiver again. After I take the shot, she holds the lime up to my lips, offering it over her shoulder.

This is fucking sexy as hell.

One more. One more for her then I'm getting her naked. I can't stand it.

She motions for me to lean back on the counter, giving her access to my stomach, and proceeds to drive me out of my fucking mind with that sweet mouth of hers. When she takes the lime from my fingers, I lean in and pull it out of her mouth with my teeth and spit it in the nearby sink, then take her face in my hands and lower my mouth to hers, finally kissing her the way I've been needing to.

She tastes like lime and tequila and pure heaven, and the next thing I know, we're stripping out of our clothes, leaving a trail to the bed. I lay her on her back. She's only wearing a scrap of black underwear.

And a come-hither smile that would tempt any saint.

Rather than covering her body with mine, I drag my hands down her torso, from her shoulders, over her breasts, her ribs, and hips. And I grip onto her panties with my teeth and pull them down her legs, then toss them over my shoulder and spread her legs wide.

"Fuck, Lila. You are gorgeous."

"You're not so bad yourself," she says breathlessly. "Can I touch you now? You're really far away."

"Not yet."

"But I'm tingly."

I smile up at her. "Tingly?"

"Mmm," she nods and closes her eyes as my fingertips glide up and down her inner thighs. "Your lips on my neck made me all tingly."

"Did the tequila help?" I ask dryly.

"Didn't need the tequila." She gasps as my fingertip finds her pink lips. She's shaved clean and wet as fuck.

"I'm going to tease you a bit," I murmur and push my finger inside her, then pull it out and push it through her folds, up to her clit and back down again, making a circle over and over. Her hands grip the sheets at her hips and the muscles in her thighs tighten.

"Asher," she groans. "Seriously."

"Seriously what?"

God, she is wet. And tight. And she's going to feel like heaven when I finally slide inside her.

"Seriously, fuck me!"

I don't need any further invitation. I lean in and latch on to her clit, pulling it into my mouth and sucking hard as I fuck her with my fingers. She jackknifes up, coming amazingly, crying out. Her hands latch onto my hair as she grinds her pussy against my mouth, riding out her orgasm.

Finally, she lets go, and I travel up her amazing body, leaving wet kisses on her torso, her nipples, her neck. I scoot her further up the bed and reach for a condom, quickly cover myself and kiss her hard as the head of my cock rests at her opening. She raises her legs, hitching them around my hips, but I pull them even higher, brace them on my shoulders, and push inside her, all the way.

"Oh. My. God." Her eyes close. Her hands grip onto my arms.

"Open your eyes," I command her and begin to move, slowly at first, as she watches me, her eyes glassy, not from the alcohol now, but from pure, unadulterated lust. My hips pick up speed. My pelvic bone hits her clit with every thrust, and I have to brace myself on the headboard for leverage.

She reaches down and presses her fingertips to her clit, making me almost fucking lose it. There is nothing hotter than watching a woman touch herself.

Unless you're fucking her while she touches herself.

She clenches around me, hard, bites her lip, and I know she's about to come. Jesus, I'm going to come with her.

"Harder," she whispers, and I gladly comply, pushing and pulling faster, a bit harder, and suddenly, the bed...*falls.*

Our gazes collide, but I don't stop.

A fucking tsunami couldn't stop me now.

I simply shift so we don't fall, holding her in place with my free arm.

"Oh my God," she whispers. "Gonna come."

"That's right, Lila. Come for me," I croon to her, on the edge myself. "Come with me."

She comes apart, squeezing me so tight I have no choice but to follow her right over the edge. I collapse on top of her, panting, sweating, and already thinking about round two when she starts to giggle beneath me.

"We broke the bed," she says and pushes her fingers into the hair at the back of my neck.

I grin and press my lips to her cheek. "We did."

She starts to laugh in earnest now. "We seriously broke the bed."

I push away from her and brush a piece of hair off her cheek. "Looks like it."

"Right on." She holds her fist up and I bump it with mine. "Good job."

I smirk and roll us onto the floor, dragging the blankets with us. "Let's try for amazing job."

Chapter One

~Lila~

"Do you have a minute, Lila?"

I glance up from the essay on Harriet Tubman that has me riveted. The student who wrote this paper did her research and clearly loves the topic. Standing in the doorway of my office is the dean of my department at Tulane University, Rick Wilson.

"Of course." I smile politely and gesture to the chair across from me. "Have a seat."

Rick, who is usually a happy, cheerful man, is sober today as he lowers into the chair. He leans forward and takes a deep breath, and I'm afraid I already know what he's going to say.

Don't say it.

"I don't think there's an easy way to tell you this, Lila."

I shake my head and close my eyes. "Who is it?"

He sighs, and I open my eyes to find him rubbing his mouth with his fingers in agitation. "Leslie Fisher."

My heart sinks as I think of the sweet, blonde girl in my Women's History class. "What happened to her?"

"The same as the other two." He sighs again and stares at me with sad eyes. "She was raped and beaten, left for dead."

My head whips up. "She's not dead?"

"She wasn't when they found her. She was taken to the hospital, but I don't have an update."

He didn't kill her!

"Maybe she'll be able to tell the police who did this." Tears fill my eyes at the horror that my student must have gone through. "Three in one month, Rick."

"I want to know what in the hell is happening on my campus," he mutters in frustration.

"That's what we would like to know as well."

Our heads whip up at the sound of a woman's voice in my doorway. She's petite, with her blonde hair in a ponytail, dressed in jeans and a simple gray T-shirt. Her eyes are hard, mouth grim.

And standing right behind her is…*Asher.*

"Can I help you?"

How are the words even coming out of my mouth? How is Asher at my office? How did he find me here?

"I'm Detective Jordan," the woman replies as she and Asher step into my office. "And this is—"

"Asher," he says, interrupting her, earning a look of surprise from his partner.

"My lieutenant," she adds. "We would like to ask you a few questions, Ms. Bailey."

I frown, still watching Asher, whose dark eyes haven't left my face. "I'm happy to answer any questions you have. Can you tell me how Leslie is?"

"No," Asher answers, his eyes narrowing just a bit. "Mr. Wilson, may we speak with Ms. Bailey alone, please?"

"Are you okay?" Rick asks me softly.

"Of course." I nod and smile reassuringly while my insides quake. *No, I'm not okay! The man I had the most incredible one-night stand with in my life just walked through my door!*

"If you'll be in your office, we will stop in and speak with you when we're done here," Asher says.

"No problem." Rick turns back to me. "Call me if you need

me."

Asher shuts the door behind Rick and takes a seat across from me while Jordan paces behind him.

"Obviously you know that young women are being murdered on campus," Jordan says.

"Yes." He's looking at me like I'm a stranger. Maybe he doesn't remember me. I mean, it was only one night. One fantastic, incredible night, but still. And we'd been drinking.

And why am I obsessing over this when young women are being killed at the university where I work? What kind of a horrible person am I?

"They're all students in your US Women's History class." Asher leans forward, bracing his elbows on his knees. "And in your weekly study group."

"Yes, they were students who were in the study group. We meet twice a week."

"Do you lead the study group personally, or do you assign an aid to do it?" Jordan asks.

"I lead it," I reply.

"Why?" she asks.

"I like working with the students. I like to be able to help them." I shrug as I think about my group of lively, funny students, and my heart hurts all over again. "Is there any news on Leslie?"

"We can't tell you that," Jordan replies softly. "I'm sorry. I know it must be hard."

"Do you know your students well?" Asher asks.

"Not all of them." I tap my finger on the desk. "But I do get to know the ones in the study group fairly well because it's such a small group. They're good kids."

"Kids who are failing your class," Asher adds.

"Not all of them." I frown. "Some of them just need the extra help. And just because they struggle doesn't mean they deserve what's happening to them."

"Of course not," Jordan agrees. "What do you know about

what's happening, Lila?"

"I've seen the news reports, of course, and heard rumors."

"Okay, what do you think you know?"

"That the girls have been raped and beaten to death, in the evening, after study group." I swallow hard and fight to keep tears at bay. "I wish I knew if Leslie was okay."

"She's not," Asher replies abruptly. "I'm sorry. She passed away during the night."

"Oh." Now I can't stop the tears. "Oh, she was just a kid."

"They're all kids," Jordan says and walks around the desk to pat my shoulder. "I'm sorry for your loss."

"Lila," Asher says, leaning forward again. "I need you to think back over the past few months and try to remember if you've seen or heard anything unusual. A person or people hanging around after your study group that shouldn't be there. Have the students mentioned anything?"

I'm shaking my head no as I try to think back. "There's been nothing suspicious," I reply. "We meet in the library, so there are always different people coming and going, but I haven't noticed anything off."

"We'd like for you to cancel the study group for the rest of the semester," Jordan says.

"No way," I reply immediately. "These kids need the help. Without it, they could fail, and I don't want that for them."

They're such good kids. Beautiful, smart, with their whole lives ahead of them. They deserve everything wonderful in the world. They should be dating and eating pizza and stressing over finals.

They shouldn't be lying in the damn morgue.

"People are being killed," Asher says, looking at me like I'm being stupid. "Canceling the group makes sense."

"We don't know for sure that he's targeting the kids in *my* group," I insist. I can hear the ridiculousness in my own ears. "Do we?"

"No," Jordan replies. "We don't have evidence of that."

"Well then, unless you do, I'm not canceling." I hold Asher's narrowed gaze with my own. "You can't make me."

"Oh, yes. I can." He sighs and rubs the back of his neck. "But I won't. For now. But come on, Lila. Be reasonable. Change the time or the place of the group."

I sigh in relief as he pulls a card out of his pocket and passes it to me. "Okay," I concede. "I'll change the days of the week that we meet. And I'll make sure they come and go in groups."

Asher nods. "I'll be in touch. But I want you to call if *anything* trips a red flag. I'm serious, Lila. Anything."

"I will," I promise.

"You look good," Asher says softly and offers me half a smile. I raise a brow in surprise.

"I didn't think you recognized me."

"Of course I did."

"You know each other?" Jordan asks with a jolt.

"It's been about a year," I reply.

"Nine months," Asher corrects me.

"You've only lived here for six," Jordan says to Asher, who just shrugs.

He moved to New Orleans?

"I'd like a list of everyone in your group," Asher says, ignoring Jordan.

"It changes a lot, depending on who needs help and when. But I can get you a list of the regulars."

"Good." He stands and follows Jordan to the door, then turns back and smiles at me. "It's good to see you, Lila."

I nod, but before I can answer, he's gone.

I immediately reach for my phone and call my best friend, Kate.

"If you're canceling lunch today, I will punch you in the neck the next time I see you."

"You know, hanging out with all those Boudreaux boys has made you really violent." I smile as I lean back in my chair, thinking of my best friend and her new family. Kate hit the mother lode when she found her Eli and his family. "And I'm not canceling, I just needed to tell you something and it won't wait for lunch."

"Okay. Shoot."

"First of all, there's been another murder, Kate. Another girl from my class."

"Oh no. Oh my gosh, I'm so sorry." At the sound of my friend's voice, I'm sad all over again. I didn't know Leslie well, but she was a happy, sweet girl.

"Me too."

"What else is going on?"

"Asher just left my office."

Silence.

"Kate?"

"Asher, of the hottest sex in the history of the world, Asher?"

You have no fucking idea, sister.

"Yes, that Asher."

"How did he find you?"

"He's the lieutenant assigned to the case. He was here to ask me questions."

"I didn't think he lived here." I can hear the frown in her voice, and the sound of her pen slapping against her desk.

"It seems he moved here about six months ago."

"Please, for the love of God, tell me you got his number."

I grin. "He gave me his card, yes."

Kate squeals on the other end of the phone, making me laugh. "Right on!"

Not that I'll ever get the guts up to call him.

Unless I get drunk again.

Maybe I should drink more often.

"It was weird. At first I didn't think he recognized me, but then toward the end he said it was good to see me."

"I like him."

"You don't know him," I reply and roll my eyes.

"He's hot. Sorry, babe," she says to Eli, who must be in the room with her, "and he has a good job. You could do worse."

"Gee, thanks." I chuckle and glance at the time. "Okay, I'll see you at lunch."

"Oh, I can't."

"What? Throat punch, Kate."

"I was actually going to cancel. I'm sorry. I had a meeting come up."

"And by *meeting* do you mean hot office sex with your ridiculously sexy billionaire boyfriend?" I ask dryly and try like mad to shove away the jealousy that spears through me.

But, come on, Eli is *hot*. And rich. And so in love with Kate it's disgusting.

"Well, there could be some of that, yes," Kate confirms with a laugh.

"You're ditching me for sex. What ever happened to *sisters before misters?*"

"Do you need me?" she asks soberly. "Because I can cancel the office sex, I mean, meeting, and still meet you."

"No." I laugh, so happy that I live close to my best friend again. "I'm okay. A little sad, but okay."

"Let's reschedule for beignets tomorrow morning," she suggests.

"Will you get out of bed early enough for that, or will Eli talk you into a meeting then too?"

"Well, I can't make any promises," she replies with a smile in her voice.

"You're disgusting. Enjoy your meeting. I'll see you in the morning."

I hang up, and suddenly all of the events from that night nine months ago come flooding back and I have to bite my lip and cross my legs at the sudden burst of pure lust that shoots through me, even making my fingertips tingle. That one night with Asher was better than all of the other nights I've had with other men combined.

The man knows his way around a woman's body.

And he lives in New Orleans now.

Chapter Two

~Asher~

"So, that was interesting," Jordan says as we jog down the steps of Lila's building on the Tulane University campus toward the parking lot.

"We didn't really find out anything we don't already know," I reply, deliberately misunderstanding her.

"Right. That's what I meant." She rolls her eyes, making my lips twitch. "For someone who's supposed to play the *bad cop*, you were sucking at it. And that's not like you. You play *bad cop* really well."

I'm not about to tell her that it took everything in me to not stalk around that desk and pull Lila into my arms and kiss the fuck out of her. Or that all I could think about while looking at her was the way she moved beneath me, the sounds she made, the way she smelled while I was deep inside her, losing my ever-loving mind.

Seeing her again was a punch in the gut. I'm surprised I was able to speak at all.

And now that I know that *my* Lila is this maniac's focus, all I can think about is tucking her away and making sure she's safe.

There's no way in hell I'm telling my partner that. I'll never live it down.

"I didn't need to play bad cop," I reply and slip my Ray-Bans on my face. "She's not a suspect."

"Not right now."

I glance down at Jordan then shake my head as we climb in my car.

"And what was up with you telling her about Leslie dying?"

"It'll be all over the news in about twenty minutes," I reply softly. "There's no reason to not tell her."

"I'm surprised you didn't tell her about the notes left on the scene too."

I scowl and throw the car out of gear before pulling out of the parking space and turning to Jordan.

"Do you have something to say?"

She sighs and shakes her head. "God, I sound like a jealous girlfriend. It's just that the sexual tension in that room was off the charts, Ash. I've never seen you like that."

"We've been partners for six months, not years. There's plenty you haven't seen."

She nods and then grins at me. "Whatever happened between you two must have been off the hook."

You have no fucking idea.

"Does your husband know that you have such a raging crush on me?" I put the car back in gear and pull out of the parking lot.

"Whatever. Don't flatter yourself. I have a hot man at home."

"If you say so." I turn toward the precinct and toss her a glance.

"Are you saying my husband *isn't* hot?" she asks as though she's offended.

"I'm a dude. I'll never say that another dude is hot."

"Well, I'm a woman, and I'm telling you he is."

"Right." I laugh and shake my head. "Back to Lila."

"Yes, back to Lila." She clears her throat, and I can tell she wants to ask questions, but instead, she just clears her throat again. "I guess you'll be stuck to her like glue."

"In light of those notes left on the scenes, yes." Rage fills me at the thought of anyone wanting to hurt Lila. And with the rage is a new emotion now that I know she's the same sweet woman that I spent one unforgettable night with last summer: Fear.

"We don't know for sure that the threats are pointed at her," Jordan says reasonably. "Her name isn't mentioned. He could mean another teacher."

I shake my head, hoping she's right, but knowing in my gut that she's not. "I don't think so. Each of the victims is from her study group. If they were just in one of her classes, I could agree that it might be a crazy coincidence. But this is too focused. All three were studying in that group minutes before they were attacked. And all three of the notes are angry. Very angry. He's making her pay for something."

"I agree," she says with a sigh. "I've seen murders before, Asher. This is New Orleans, after all. But I've never seen anything quite this...*evil*."

I nod.

"Have you?" she asks.

I nod again, slowly. "Once."

"In Seattle?"

"Yes. We had a serial killer there about four years ago." *And the motherfucker destroyed my life.* "He killed eight women before we caught him."

"What's up with the serial killers in Seattle? Is it all the rain that sends people over the edge?" She bites her thumbnail and looks out the passenger window.

"There are no more killers in Seattle than other parts of the country."

"Hello. Green River Killer. He killed, like, eight hundred women. That counts for a lot."

"Good point," I mutter and think back on the man four years ago who made the Green River Killer look like a Boy

Scout troop leader.

There is no way in hell that anything like that will touch Lila.

"So, you're going to look out for Lila," Jordan says, mirroring my thoughts.

"Yes. I'm going to stick close to her. This fucker isn't going to touch her."

I glance over to find Jordan watching me thoughtfully. "How well do you know Lila, Asher?"

"Not well," I reply truthfully.

"You seem pretty passionate about keeping her safe for someone who doesn't know her well."

I shrug a shoulder as we get stopped in traffic. "It's my job to keep her safe."

"Right." She nods once and is smart enough to not say any more.

Lila.

I cursed myself as an idiot for months after our night together for not getting her number, or at least her last name. I wanted to call her, to see her again, but she told me she lived in Denver, and God knows that trying to maintain a long distance relationship is next to impossible.

But she lives *here*.

Yes, I'll be sticking very close to Lila, and not just because it's my job. From the minute she fell into my lap on that airplane, my hands have itched to touch her. Running into her again in that bar was the best stroke of luck I've ever had, and that night with her was off the fucking charts.

I can't resist her. For the first time in *years*, I don't want to resist her.

I simply want *her*.

* * * *

"Daddy! My purple shirt is dirty!"

I swear ripely as the toast pops up in the toaster, burnt to a damn crisp, and lean on the countertop, my head down, praying for patience.

"You wore the purple shirt yesterday," I remind her as she bounces into the kitchen of our small townhouse and wrinkles her adorable little freckle-covered nose.

"You burned it again."

"I know."

"I like the purple shirt."

"You can't wear it every day." I kiss the top of her head and toss the black bread into the garbage, ready to start over. "Aren't you going to be late for school?"

"No, it's Thursday." She rolls her eyes, looking suddenly much older than her ten years, making me smile. "It's late start day at school."

"Your favorite day of the week." I pick her up off her feet and set her on the countertop where I can look her in her gorgeous green eyes. Eyes the same color as her mother's. "How are you, bubba?"

"Good." She giggles and holds her fist up for a fist-bump, which she seems to suddenly think is the funnest thing *ever*. Especially the explosion part. "I need my purple shirt."

She sticks her lower lip out and bats her eyelashes at me.

Damn it, she's adorable.

"That doesn't work on me," I lie.

"Please?" She grips my cheeks in her small hands and pulls my face to hers, leaning her forehead against mine playfully. "I love you, Daddy." She's staring me in the eyes.

"I love you too." My lips twitch, and I want to laugh, but I'm very proud of myself for standing firm.

"May I please wear my purple shirt?"

"No."

"But Masie will be wearing purple, and I promised that I would wear purple too, and that's the only purple shirt I have!"

God, give me patience.

"Enough." I kiss her forehead and lift her onto her feet. "Find another shirt. Masie will not die of disappointment."

"No, but I might," she says with a scowl.

"Hello?" Franny calls out as she lets herself in the front door. "Sorry I'm running late. This morning sickness is ridiculous."

I smile at the pretty blonde woman my brother had the sense to marry and kiss her on the cheek.

"You're fine. It's late start today, and I don't have to be to work for a while yet. In fact, if you have things handled here, I'll go for a run."

"Daddy won't let me wear my purple shirt," Casey says, ratting me out to her aunt.

"You wore it yesterday," Franny says, making me smile and Casey deflate in defeat. "Besides, he's the boss. What he says goes."

"When do I get to be the boss?" Casey asks, folding her arms over her chest.

"When you grow up and start paying your own bills," I reply. "So, you okay here?"

"Maybe." Fran leans on the countertop and crosses her arms, studying me with pure calculation on her pretty features.

"Okay."

"Does this run take you past Café du Monde?"

"It can."

"Beignets!" Casey exclaims and claps, bouncing on her feet, the purple shirt clearly forgotten. "Can we have some? Please?"

"Maybe," I reply with a laugh, but when I turn to walk away, Fran grips my arm in her small but surprisingly strong grasp.

"You don't understand. I'm pregnant, and this baby wants beignets. Today." She points to her still flat belly, mutiny in her eyes. "Do we understand each other, Smith?"

"You just assaulted an officer."

"I'm married to an officer. You don't scare me."

"Beignets!" Casey shouts and high-fives Fran.

"Well, I'd be a stupid man to try to come between a pregnant woman and food."

"And you're not stupid, my friend," she replies with a satisfied smile. "Plus, you'll be the baby's favorite uncle."

"I'm already the favorite uncle."

"Bring those beignets, and yes, you are."

I laugh as I jog upstairs to my bedroom, quickly change into a tank and shorts, lace my shoes, plug my earphones in my ears and set out.

The French Quarter is a few miles from our townhouse, which is the perfect distance for a run. Fall Out Boy blasts in my ears as my feet pound on the concrete. The sidewalks are uneven, making me watch my step carefully. It's a gorgeous early spring day, warm and sunny. The sunlight filters through the leaves of the massive oak trees that line the boulevards.

This city is not only rich in history, but it's just plain beautiful. Moving here last fall was the best thing for both Casey and myself. She made friends quickly in school, and with Fran and Mike so close by, I never have to worry about who is going to help out with her.

And with a promotion from detective to lieutenant, I can't complain a bit about my job. I enjoy the work here more than I ever have.

The music in my ears stops as my phone begins to ring. Without breaking my stride, I answer while pulling my tank off and tucking it into my shorts at my waist, letting it hang over my hip.

"Smith."

"Do not tell me you're having sex," Matt, my former partner from Seattle, says.

"I'm running, asshole." I grin as I cross Canal Street, over the tracks, into the French Quarter. "What's up with you?"

"I'm just checking on you. How are things in the Big Easy?"

"Busy."

"It's kind of weird to have you breathing heavy in my ear," Matt complains, his voice completely serious, but I can just imagine him grinning.

"We used to run together all the time."

"Yeah, but the heavy breathing wasn't *in* my ear."

"How's the family?" I ask. "How's Nic?"

"She's gorgeous."

"I know that," I reply. "I'm glad she finally made an honest man of you."

He chuckles. "We might come down there, spend a few days in a couple weeks."

"Look, man, I'm sorry I missed the wedding." I grimace. "If this fucker hadn't started killing these girls right before—"

"I get it. It's fine." And I know he means it, but regret hangs heavily in my gut. I love Matt, as if he was my own brother, and Casey and I both adore Nic, his new wife, as well. I was looking forward to their wedding.

But, duty called.

Duty always calls.

"So, what brings you to New Orleans?"

"Neither of us has ever been. I want to get away for a few days and we don't have time to go out of the country. With her bakery, and the force, we can't take that much time off of work."

"Will she bring some cupcakes with her?" I ask with a smile. God, that woman can bake. "Casey would love it."

"Don't bullshit me. *You* would love it."

"Tomato/tom-ah-to," I reply.

"I'll mention it to her. What dates work?"

"Nothing works. I'll make it work, though. I'm in the middle of a serial case. Maybe I can bounce some ideas off you."

"The Tulane University case?" he asks with surprise.

"You've heard of it?"

"A serial killer makes the national news, partner." I grin at the nickname. "Don't worry about us. Just make time for dinner. We can show ourselves around."

"I'll make time," I reply as I approach the green and white awning of Café du Monde. Sitting at a table at the edge of the seating area is a pretty redhead and gorgeous brunette, and I smile widely as I slow down to a walk. "I have to go, partner. Just e-mail me the details. Looking forward to seeing you."

"Me too. See you soon."

I end the call and approach the wrought iron railing that the girls are sitting next to, their heads together, talking and nibbling on beignets.

Lila licks her lips and my dick immediately stirs to life.

I want to feel that tongue on me.

"Good morning, ladies."

They both look up in surprise. Kate smiles, and Lila's mouth drops open as her eyes roam up and down my naked torso, making me chuckle.

She likes what she sees.

Which is damn convenient because she's about to see a lot of me.

Chapter Three

~Lila~

"These should be illegal," Kate says and takes a bite of her piping-hot, powdered sugar-covered nugget of deliciousness. I simply nod in agreement because my mouth is too full of my own nugget of deliciousness to speak.

When I finally swallow and take a drink of my coffee, I lick my lips and smile at my friend. "Thanks for tearing yourself away from sexy Eli to have breakfast with me."

"I don't have to be with him 24/7," she says with a roll of the eyes. "Besides, he had to leave early for a morning meeting."

"So things are still going well?" I ask before taking another bite.

"Yep," she replies. "We have our moments when we want to strangle each other, which I assume is normal when you live with someone, but then we just have crazy awesome sex and all is better."

I laugh. "Well, here's to crazy hot sex." I salute her and take a sip of coffee. "Not that I remember."

"That's your own fault," Kate says. "You could so get laid."

"I'm not exactly the one-night stand type, and I don't have time to date."

"Bullshit and bullshit."

"Excuse me?"

"You had a one-night stand with Asher, and you *do* have time to date, you just choose not to."

"My job takes up a lot of my time," I insist and glance over at a man as he starts to play his saxophone not too far away. "And I don't *usually* do the one-night stand thing. I'm way too responsible for that."

"Everyone's job takes up a lot of time," Kate says and waves me off as if I'm being ridiculous. "It's all about priorities. If seeing someone is important, you'll make room for him." She tosses me her sly Cheshire cat grin and pulls another beignet apart before popping part of it in her mouth. "And now that Asher is back, you can make room for him."

"I knew you were going to start with this."

"What's wrong with Asher?"

"Nothing." *Not even one thing.* I stop talking and can't help the smile that slips on my lips. "God, nothing is wrong with him. You saw him."

"I rest my case."

"But just because we had one hot night together doesn't mean I should start dating him. I don't even know that he's still single." And if he's taken, he should be ashamed of himself for the way he looked at me yesterday.

"We don't know that he's not," she reminds me. "God, you're cynical when it comes to men."

"Hello, pot."

"I'm not cynical. I had reasons for my trust issues."

I cover Kate's hand with mine, already sorry for my remark. "I know. And I have my reasons for being cynical."

"A deadbeat dad and an absent mom are not the best reasons to be cynical."

I bust out laughing at the ridiculousness of that statement. "I think those are two very good reasons, actually."

"You aren't your parents."

"You're right. I'm not an alcoholic pothead or an irresponsible woman without a maternal bone in her body."

"No, you're neither of those things. You're so much better than that." She takes another bite. "Look, you can't stay celibate your whole life."

I frown at that thought.

"It's been so long since I had sex, I don't even know if my vagina still works," I admit in a whisper, making Kate laugh.

"Trust me, it works."

"How do you know?"

She simply continues to laugh.

"Good morning, ladies."

Our heads both whip up at the deep, sexy voice, and I'm suddenly staring at a very sweaty, very half-naked, Asher.

Oh Jesus.

"Good morning," Kate says beside me, but I'm not paying attention to the words they're saying. My mouth goes dry at the sight of Asher's naked torso. He's wearing running shorts, with his shirt tucked into the waist at his hip. He has earbuds in his ears, leading to his phone in his pocket.

He's panting from his run, and sweat is running down his forehead, his cheek.

His fucking amazing chest.

One drop of sweat slowly makes its way down his sternum to his chiseled abs, and it takes everything in me to not lean over and lick it off.

Down, girl.

"Lila?"

"What?"

Asher's eyes are laughing as he props his hands on his hips, watching me. "How are you?"

"Oh, I'm fine."

Kate snickers beside me, earning a kick to the shin from me.

"You look amazing," he replies and offers me that half-smile. The one that promises all kinds of amazing naughtiness and has kept me up many a night over the past nine months.

"Thank you," I murmur. Why am I so shy with him now? That night at the bar, I was confident. I knew exactly what I wanted, and that was him. I wasn't shy. I didn't hesitate.

And now I feel tongue-tied and *hot*.

Probably because now I know what he's capable of.

"I'm coming to your study group tonight," he says as he pops the earbuds out of his ears.

"Why?" I ask with surprise.

"I'm going to escort you home."

"Oh, that's so nice," Kate says with a dreamy sigh, and I roll my eyes at her.

"That's not necessary," I reply. "I'll be fine."

"In case you missed it, there's a killer out there, Lila," Asher says, his handsome face perfectly serious now. His jaw is square and strong, and covered in just a little black stubble. His hair is a complete sweaty mess. He's half naked.

He's the sexiest thing I've ever seen, and yet just those few words out of his mouth have my blood running cold.

"I'll be there," he repeats before I can say anything. He smiles again and winks at Kate, then pins me in his hot stare once more. "I need to get some beignets home to Casey."

"Who's Casey?" Kate asks before I can.

"My daughter." He backs away, watching me, and I'm struck dumb. "I'll see you tonight." And with that, he saunters away.

"He has a daughter," I say when he's out of earshot.

"Sounds like it," Kate replies with a nod.

"Holy fuck," I whisper, suddenly mortified. "He's married!"

"We don't know that," Kate says with a frown.

"Hello? He has a daughter."

"So he said."

"I had sex with a *married man*." I swallow, mortified. "I'm a home wrecker."

"Okay, stop." Kate waves her hands in front of her, getting my attention. "He said he was taking beignets home to *Casey*. Not his family, or his wife, or to *them*. Just to her."

"Maybe he didn't want to hurt my feelings."

"Lila." Kate pushes her fingers on her eyebrows, as if I'm giving her a headache. "He could be divorced. Widowed. Maybe he *never* married the mother. Maybe she left as soon as the baby was born."

"Oh God." I frown and immediately feel sorry for the little girl. I can see her in my head, a sweet brunette girl who looks just like her daddy, crying and pining for her mother who abandoned her as a baby. "Wait. I'm getting very dramatic here."

"Yes." Kate nods. "Stop it. He's probably divorced."

"Right."

"And he's clearly still interested in you," she adds and sips the last of her coffee.

I shrug one shoulder, as if it doesn't matter. "He has a kid."

"So?"

"I don't do kids," I remind her. "I don't want kids, and I certainly don't get involved with men with kids."

Because as much as that little voice in the back of my head tells me that having a child of my own would be the most amazing thing in the world, I just can't take the chance that I would be as big a failure as my own parents were.

"Get over yourself," Kate says as she rolls her eyes. "Stop focusing on what you *won't* do. Because maybe you will."

Right.

"Maybe not."

"Such a Debbie Downer. Nobody wants to fuck a Debbie Downer."

"I'm just being realistic. I'm responsible, remember?"

"You're kind of a pain in the ass. He's nice. He's hot. Maybe you can just do the friends with benefits thing. No harm, no foul."

"Oh. You could be onto something."

Kate smiles smugly. "I'm a smart one."

* * * *

He's been wandering through the library for the past thirty minutes, waiting for me to finish with my group, and making it very hard to focus on my students.

And that kind of pisses me off.

If these kids are taking the time to be here, I need to be here.

"Okay guys, you're doing great," I say as they begin to filter out of the small study room that I have on reserve for us twice a week. "I'll see you in class on Monday. And remember what I said! Be safe out there."

"I so appreciate your help, Lila," Colin says. This is the second semester in a row that he's had to take this class. I hated having to fail him last semester, and I'm so happy that he's doing better now. He's a good kid. Friendly with the other students, happy-go-lucky. He's small in stature, with a shaved head, smiling eyes, and always quick to make a joke.

We all enjoy him.

"You're welcome," I reply with a smile. "You're doing so much better, Colin."

"Well, as much as I like you, I'd rather not take the same class again."

"I understand."

"Thanks Lila." Cheyenne, a pretty girl with short, bleach blonde hair says as she walks out. "See you Monday."

"Travel in groups! It's dangerous out there!"

"I'll walk her to her car," Colin offers with a wink and drapes his arm around Cheyenne's shoulders. "You're safe with me, cupcake."

The students are all gone as I close my computer and put it

in my bag, along with a pen and the scarf I had on earlier but had to take off when it got too warm. I flip off the light and close the door behind me as Asher approaches from across the library.

God, the way he moves should come with a warning label.

Warning: May cause brain loss during movement.

He moves effortlessly, as though he's completely comfortable in his own skin. And he should be.

His skin is pretty damn impressive.

His dark hair is messy, as usual, as though he's been shoving his fingers through it. He shaved the stubble off his chin, probably when he showered after his run.

He's dressed in jeans and a black T-shirt, and I want to rip them off of him. Right here, right now.

What the hell is up with my hormones?

He has a daughter!

And probably a wife.

"Hey," he says with a smile.

"You really don't have to walk me home," I reply. "It's not far."

"It's not here in the library, is it?"

I smirk. "Of course not."

"Then I need to walk you home," he replies and places his hand on the small of my back as he leads me out of the library. He takes my computer bag from me and carries it for me.

And if he wasn't married, that might be the swooniest thing I've ever seen.

"It's nice tonight," I comment as we walk across campus and into the nearby neighborhood where my apartment is. "It's warming up."

"It is," he agrees. "Summer will be here before we know it."

"This is me." I gesture to my building and take my bag from him. "I'll be fine from here."

"I'd like to walk you in," he replies seriously. I glance up to see his mouth firm.

"Why?"

"I want to make sure your place is empty."

I roll my eyes. "Look, I understand that young girls are being killed, and it's heartbreaking and horrific, but I hardly think that the killer is waiting for me in my apartment."

"Lila." He stops me on the sidewalk and takes my shoulders in his hands, his hot gaze on mine. "There are things happening with this investigation that I can't tell you about. I need you to trust me. I need you to cooperate with me."

"Okay." I back out of his touch, making him frown. "But your wife might have an issue with you coming into my apartment. Especially after last summer."

I turn to walk ahead of him, but he pulls me to a stop again, and this time he looks...*angry*.

And maybe a little confused.

"I'm not married."

I blink, but before I can speak, he continues.

"Did you think that because I mentioned Casey this morning that I'm married?"

I shrug.

"I'm a single dad." And with that he turns and walks ahead of me.

"I'm sorry."

"It's fine." But then he stops again and scowls at me. "No, it's not fine. Do you seriously think that I'd fuck you the way I did last summer if I were married?"

"I don't know you." I'm surprisingly calm now that I know that he's *not* married. "It's not like we've actually had conversations about ourselves."

"Well, let me make myself perfectly clear; I'm not a cheater. Casey's mom is gone. I'm not married. I don't have a girlfriend."

"Okay." I nod as he steps a little closer. He drags his fingertips down my cheek, but doesn't kiss me. He's really good at the sexy, get really close and make me want it thing.

And he's single.

Thank God.

"Let's get you inside," he whispers and kisses my forehead, sending electricity from my head to my feet, then takes my hand and leads me to my door. "Stay here."

"Asher—"

"Stay here," he repeats, and waits for me to unlock the door before he walks in, leaving me on my doorstep.

This is ridiculous.

I step inside and shut the door, toss my purse and keys on the nearby table, and lay my computer bag on the dining room table.

"So help me God, Delila, if you don't start listening to me, I'll spank your ass."

I twirl at his angry voice, my jaw dropped. "Excuse me?"

"You heard me."

"One: how do you know my full name?"

"I'm leading this investigation. I know more about you than you're probably comfortable with."

Well, that fucking sucks.

"Two: try to spank my ass and I'll knock you on yours."

His lips twitch. "Good girl."

"You're an arrogant ass."

"I'm not arrogant, I'm doing my best to keep you safe." He advances on me and pins me against the door, his hands flat on the wood, on either side of my head, his mouth inches from mine, stealing the breath from my lungs. "Nothing is going to happen to you, Lila."

"I'm safe, Asher."

"Yes, you are. I'm making sure of it." Just when I expect him to kiss the ever-loving hell out of me, he gently cups my face in his hands, his thumbs trace circles on my cheeks, and he lowers his face to mine. He nibbles the corner of my mouth sweetly. "I've dreamed of this mouth," he whispers.

My hands find their way to his ribcage, bunching his T-shirt in my fists.

Jesus, I want to fucking climb him.

"The chemistry between us is crazy," I reply.

"I know." He swallows hard and kisses down my jaw to my ear. "You're so damn beautiful, Delila."

"I hate my name," I whisper.

"Why?"

"Because it's an old lady name."

"I love your name."

God, he's intoxicating me. I'm numb from the pleasure, and yet, I'm more sensitive than I've ever been.

And that doesn't make any sense.

None of this makes any sense.

"I want to spend tomorrow with you."

I open my eyes to find his on me, narrowed just a little. His hand has drifted down my side to my hip, but he's still holding the other side of my face in his strong hand.

"To protect me?" I ask.

"That's only part of it." He kisses me chastely. "I want to be with you. Do you have tomorrow off for the holiday?"

"Yes." I give a little nod. "Okay."

"Okay." He kisses me one more time, bites my lower lip, then takes a deep breath and leans his forehead on my shoulder. "I have to go. Lock this door and stay smart, Lila. I'll be back in the morning."

"Okay."

"Oh, and I'll have Casey with me." He winks. "You'll like her."

"Oh. Okay."

Is okay all I know how to say?

I watch as he leaves, lock the door behind him, and take a deep, cleansing breath. Dear sweet Jesus, that man is potent. And he's a good guy.

A good guy with a kid.

The thought would normally scare me, but I feel a smile spread across my face at the thought of watching him with a little girl. Does she have him wrapped around her finger? How is he with her?

I'm suddenly looking forward to tomorrow.

Chapter Four

~Asher~

"Is Lila your girlfriend?" Casey asks as we drive from our townhouse to Lila's apartment. I grin at her in the rearview.

"No. She's a friend." How do I explain to my daughter that Lila is so much more than a friend, but not my girlfriend, when I don't even understand it yet myself? I've never introduced Casey to a woman that I'm interested in. No one has ever made me consider keeping them around for the long haul, and I'm not going to bring someone into Casey's life just to have them say good-bye again.

But I actually *want* Casey to meet Lila, and that has me more than just a tad nervous.

"And why are we hanging out with her today?"

"Because I'm looking after her for a little while. You'll like her. She's nice."

"Is she nice enough to maybe eventually be your girlfriend?" she asks hopefully.

I simply chuckle, my heart hitching a bit at the longing in Casey's pretty green eyes, and park in front of Lila's building, then lead Casey up to Lila's door.

I knock and scowl when Lila opens the door without even asking who is on the other side.

"What if I had been the bad guy?"

"*Are* you the bad guy?" she asks with one brow raised, and damn if I don't want to kiss that smirk right off her gorgeous face.

"He's the good guy," Casey replies seriously.

"You must be Casey," Lila says with a smile and holds her hand out to shake my daughter's. "I'm Lila."

"You're pretty," Casey says.

"You're prettier," Lila replies as she grabs her handbag and keys. "Do you know where we're going?"

"Breakfast," Casey says and glances up at me for confirmation.

"Breakfast," I agree.

"Perfect. I'm starving." Lila offers her hand to Casey, and together they walk hand in hand toward the car.

Watching them together, the tall, slim brunette and my small, slim redhead, makes my heart catch.

I've never imagined bringing a woman into our lives full time. Casey is happy and well adjusted the way things are, and asking her to accept someone new has always seemed rather selfish of me.

It never occurred to me that she might need, or even want, a woman in our lives.

And damn if Lila doesn't look perfectly comfortable with my daughter.

"Do you have a place in mind?" Lila asks, and she and Casey climb into the car and buckle themselves in.

"I do." I grin at her and wink as I back out of the parking lot. "You'll see."

There's a little hole-in-the-wall joint not far from Lila's place that Casey and I love. It's busy today, but we're quickly shown to a table in the back corner with a view of the street. I sit with my back to the window, as always, with Casey next to me so I can keep an eye on the room.

I never sit with my back to a room.

"They have the *best* pancakes," Casey announces, setting her menu aside. "May I please have bacon with mine, Daddy?"

"Of course," I reply and kiss her head, then glance up to find Lila watching us.

"How old are you, Casey?" she asks.

"Ten," Casey replies and sips her water. "I'll be eleven in seven months and one week."

"That soon?" Lila asks with a laugh. "What grade are you in?"

"Fourth."

"Lila is a teacher," I tell Casey.

"What grade do you teach?"

"I am a college professor," Lila says.

"Wow. You must be really smart."

She's brilliant.

Lila laughs and orders pancakes and bacon for herself and Casey when the waitress arrives.

"Make it three," I say.

"You have very pretty hair," Lila tells Casey, who preens from the compliment.

"It's just like my mom's," Casey says innocently, and the stab to my heart is immediate. It's lessened with time, thankfully, but in these simple moments, it catches me off guard. "It's really curly. And red." She wrinkles her nose.

"That explains it," Lila says, looking at me with surprised eyes. "I was expecting you to have dark hair like your daddy."

"Nope. I got the red." Casey sighs. "And the freckles."

"You know, my best friend has red hair and freckles, and she's just as gorgeous as you are."

Casey smiles up at me, then back at Lila. "Cool."

"So what are our plans for the rest of the day? Surely you don't intend to try to entertain me all day." Lila takes a sip of her water, watching me over the rim.

"I do intend to entertain you all day. And don't call me Shirley."

Lila laughs, a happy, loud laugh that makes my stomach clench. She tosses her hair over one shoulder and shakes her head at me. "You're silly."

"He's really silly," Casey agrees and claps her hands as our pancakes and bacon are served. "But he's handsome. Don't you think?"

"She's really subtle," I inform Lila dryly. She simply pours maple syrup on her pancakes, so much that I wince and then chuckle at her. "Do you want some pancakes with your syrup?"

"Maybe." She winks at me and turns her attention back to Casey. "Yes, your daddy is handsome."

"And he's smart. And he has a good job. And he can fix things."

"Really?" Lila takes a bite of her bacon and leans in like Casey is about to tell her all of life's secrets. "What can he fix?"

I watch Casey, also interested to hear what it is, exactly, that I can fix.

"Well, he unclogged the toilet when I accidently dropped his phone in it and flushed."

"Oh my."

"And our stove stopped working and he replaced the lelement, and now it works again."

"I replaced the heating element in the oven," I correct her, but she's ignoring me.

"And at Christmas time, half of the lights on our Christmas tree wouldn't light, but he figured it out and made them come back on!"

"That is impressive."

I chuckle and munch on my bacon, enjoying the banter between these two amazing girls. Casey is chattering about my skills in painting the living room, clearly trying to convince Lila that she and I should be together forever, and Lila is listening. Not half-assed the way some adults do when they're humoring a kid and want to get on with their day.

Casey has Lila's undivided attention, and it terrifies me to realize that she just...*fits.*

Which is ridiculous because I hardly know her. One night in bed with her and a few conversations does not a life-long relationship make.

And yet, I know she's smart. So much smarter than me. She's kind. She's funny.

And fuck me, she's sexy as I don't know what.

And seeing her here, with my kid, she's attentive and sweet.

A man could fall in love with her.

Where the hell did that come from?

"I have a joke!" Casey announces.

"Okay, shoot," Lila says.

"Why did the peach go out with the prune?"

"Why?" Lila and I ask at the same time.

"Because it couldn't find a date!"

Casey busts out laughing. "Get it?"

"Yes," I reply, chuckling, and catch Lila's humor-filled gaze with my own. "You're a funny girl."

"This was delicious," Lila says as she lays her napkin on her empty plate. "You were right. Best pancakes ever."

"They're pretty good," I agree. "When I was a kid, my mom—"

"I have to tell you about Masie!" Casey says, interrupting me.

"Hey." I give her the *Dad Stink Eye.* "I understand that you're enjoying Lila's company, but that's no reason to be rude. Apologize please."

"I'm sorry for being rude," Casey says. "Excuse me, Daddy?"

"Yes."

"May I please tell Lila about Masie?"

My phone buzzes in my pocket as Lila laughs. "Yes, go ahead and tell her."

Casey begins to chatter about her best friend as I answer. "What's up?"

"We have another one." Jordan's voice is clipped, and I can hear road noise as she drives. "I'm on my way to the scene now."

"On my way." I motion for the waitress and pay the bill without looking at it. "We have to go, girls."

"What's wrong?" Lila asks. I hold her gaze and shake my head quickly. I won't discuss the details of my job around my daughter. She knows that I investigate murders, that I catch the bad guys, but that's it. I see things that no ten-year-old should ever be privy to.

"I have to drop you home, then take Casey to my brother's and get to work."

"I thought you had today off," Casey says with a sigh. "Did someone die?"

"Yes, baby." I kiss her head as we walk to the car. "I'm sorry."

"You don't need to make the extra trip. You can leave Casey with me."

"Are you sure?"

"Really?" Casey says excitedly. "Oh, that would be so cool."

"I'm sure," Lila says with a smile, but her eyes are worried as she lays her hand on my arm. "Is it what I think it is?"

"I'm not sure," I lie. I don't want to tell her anything until I see the scene and find out exactly what's going on. "Could be."

Lila simply nods and sits back in the seat with a sigh, her hands tightly clasped in her lap. I take one of her hands in mine and kiss her knuckles.

"It's going to be okay."

She nods and I glance in the rearview at my daughter, who is watching us carefully with a wide grin on her perfect face. She gives me a thumbs-up and winks, as though she's my buddy, and I can't help but laugh.

God save me from ten-year-old matchmakers.

* * * *

I approach the scene, a small apartment on the edge of Tulane University campus. There is yellow *DO NOT CROSS* tape everywhere. Men in uniform are directing people away from the building. Girls are crying, sitting on the curb.

Jordan rushes over to me.

"Have you gone in?" I ask as we walk briskly to the apartment where the vic was killed.

"No, I was waiting for you."

We're gloving up as we approach the door. No one is inside. "Who secured the scene?"

"I did, sir." A young uniformed officer is standing near the open doorway. He swallows hard as I approach. His nametag reads Tanner.

"Did anyone disturb the scene, Tanner?"

"I don't think so, sir. The victim's friend called it in when she arrived to take Ms. Roberts to coffee. They had a date."

"Did she touch anything?"

"She denied touching anything. She walked in, saw the vic, and called 911. She was standing here when we arrived. I made a visual confirmation that the victim was deceased, sealed the door, and called it in."

"Good job." I nod, break the seal of the yellow tape on the door, and walk inside, Jordan right behind me. She has her camera out, already taking photos of the tiny apartment.

"Do we know if she lived alone?"

"The friend confirmed that she lived alone," Tanner says from the doorway. He's young, but he's smart and respectful.

He has potential.

"Where is the vic?"

"In the bedroom." Tanner swallows hard. "It's pretty gruesome, sir."

Jordan and I look at each other and walk to the bedroom.

"Sonofabitch," Jordan whispers as we take in the scene

before us. There is blood spatter everywhere—the walls, the floor, the furniture. Even the ceiling.

The victim, Cheyenne Roberts, is lying on the bed facedown. I remember her from last night when she left the library. A pretty young blonde. Happy. Carefree.

So fucking young.

I doubt her own parents would recognize her now. Her face has been torn off. Her fingers cut off at the knuckles.

And her intestines are strung from one side of the room to the other.

Jesus Christ, what the ever-loving fuck? Why didn't I shut that damn group down? Or escort all of the girls home myself?

"Oh my God, Asher."

"Take photos, Jordan."

She swallows hard, then pulls herself together and begins to systematically work the scene with me, taking photos, sweeping for any clues. There's nothing I can see. Nothing but blood and tissue and absolute horror.

Except for the note, covered in blood. The handwriting is likely the victim's, just like the previous three.

Do you see what happens to know-it-all bitches, Lila? Bitches who think they're better than everyone else? They get their fucking face ripped off. I hope you enjoy the last few days of your pitiful life because I'm about to end it.

Jordan snaps photos of the note before I seal it up and pray there is a print on it.

But there won't be.

This fucker is careful.

"The ME just arrived," Tanner calls from the living room. "Are you ready for him?"

"Send him in," I confirm. Pierce, the best Medical Examiner in Louisiana, steps into the room and swears ripely.

"Poor girl," he says with a sigh. "What the fuck, Asher?"

"My sentiments exactly," I reply. "Can you give me a TOD?"

He nods and works his magic, testing her body temperature. "She's been dead for roughly twelve hours."

"Not long after study group," I murmur. "We're done with her. I want a full sweep after you take the body. Prints, hair, everything. If there's something here, I want it."

I march out of the apartment, rage boiling in me. "I'll meet you at the office. I want those pictures printed right away so we can add them to the board. We're missing something. We're starting from the beginning."

Jordan nods and walks to her car as I walk to mine, climb in, and speed all the way back to the office. I need to look at my notes.

He's getting more violent. More *angry*.

I'm stalking through to my office when my phone rings.

"Captain, I'm walking into my office right now."

"I want a report, in my office, in an hour."

"You'll have it."

I end the call and hold on to my temper by the skin of my teeth as Jordan joins me, shutting the door behind her, the new crime scene photos in her hands, which she passes to me and I begin to add them to the murder board I have in the center of the room, covered in photos and notes on the previous victims.

"She was twenty-one," Jordan says as she reads the report on her iPad. "Sociology major. Decent grades. No boyfriend that we know of."

"Where is she from?"

"Excuse me?"

I turn to look at her. "Her hometown."

"Shreveport," Jordan replies. "What are you thinking?"

"I'm thinking that we're missing something. Maybe the connection is as simple as being from the same town."

"Asher, the connection is Lila."

I prop my hands on my hips and stare at the photos of four girls who shouldn't be dead. My heart stills at Lila's name.

"Asher."

"I know."

"Are you going to be able to handle this? After everything you went through with your wife—"

"My wife doesn't have anything to do with this."

But Jesus Christ, I can't go through losing someone else to a maniac.

"You know what I mean."

"Are you saying I can't do my fucking job?" I spin and glare at her. "I'm doing the job, Jordan."

"I'm not saying that. But it's clear that you have feelings for Lila."

"Is it?"

"Crystal." She shakes her head and leans her hip on my desk. "She needs to be told about the notes."

"No."

"Asher, he named her specifically. He threatened her. She needs to know so she can protect herself."

"I'm protecting her."

"God, you're stubborn. Telling her about the notes—"

"Will only terrify her."

"It would terrify me," she agrees. "But if I found out later that you'd withheld that information from me, I'd be mighty pissed off."

I sigh and rub the back of my neck. "You're right. I don't like it, but you're right."

"If you weren't in love with her, I wouldn't have to talk you into telling her."

"I'm not in love with her." I smirk and shake my head.

"Right. That's why you're rubbing your heart right now."

I glance down, surprised to find that I am, indeed, rubbing my aching heart. The thought of anything happening to her sends a panic through me that I haven't felt in four years.

It's terrifying.

And she and my daughter are alone right now.

"Get comfortable," I say and pull my phone out of my pocket. "We're going to be here a while. I want to go back to the very beginning and read every report, every note all over again while we wait for the ME and crime scene reports to come in."

"You okay?"

"Just do the job, Jordan."

She nods as I dial Mike's number. "Hey, man."

"Hey, I need you to do me a favor."

Chapter Five

~Lila~

"I love peanut butter sandwiches," Casey informs me as she nibbles on her sandwich, sans crust, with her little fingers propped up to keep her drying nails from getting messed up. "And this nail polish is so pretty!"

"I love it too." I finish my sandwich and sit back on the couch, watching the sweet girl as she eats delicately. "Thanks for letting me polish your nails."

"Are you kidding? This is great! Can we play in your makeup?"

I have a moment of panic as I think of the expensive stash of makeup in my drawers, and then figure, why not? You only live once.

"Sure. Let's go." I lead Casey into my bathroom and spread eye shadows, blush, liners, mascara, and lipstick on the countertop. Her pretty green eyes widen at my loot.

"Wow," she says reverently. "You don't look like you wear that much makeup."

"That's the secret." I wink at her and study her coloring, wanting to choose just the right shades for her. "You don't want to look like you wear a lot. You choose colors that accentuate what you already have."

"You're smart."

I laugh and choose an eye shadow. "I've just been doing this for a really long time."

"Can I do you after you do me?"

"I'm already wearing makeup."

"You could take it off," she says.

"True. Okay, I'll take it off." I grab my makeup remover and wipe off my eye makeup, then smile at Casey.

"Awesome." I boost her up onto the counter so she's eye level with me, making it easier to work, and choose a brush.

"Close your eyes."

She complies and sits still as I brush eye shadow on her eyes, add liner, mascara and blush. I don't want her dad to show up and think that I've turned his daughter into a harlot.

But playing with makeup is fun. Hell, I loved playing with it at her age. I still do.

"So, you're definitely a girlie girl," I comment.

"Yes. Do you have glitter?"

I chuckle and reach for a bronzer with sparkles in it. "Glitter coming right up."

"Right on." She offers me her fist to bump, and I comply with a laugh just as my phone pings with an incoming text.

Asher: Thanks for helping me out. Not sure how long I'll be here, so my brother Mike is going to stop by and get Casey. It's okay to open the door to him.

I just love how he's now dictating who I can open the door to.

"That's your dad. Your uncle Mike is going to come get you."

"Already?" she asks with distress. "But we're having a spa day!"

My lips twitch. "You're right. I'll take care of it."

Can you give us at least an hour? We are having a spa day. And don't get mad at me for putting makeup on her.

"You're really pretty," Casey says as she watches me text.

"Like, *really* pretty."

"Thank you, sweetheart."

No problem. Thank you for being so patient.

There is no need to be patient with this adorable girl. She's funny and smart and enjoys the same things I do. Why would I need to be patient with her?

My pleasure. Really.

I tuck my phone away and make the finishing touches on Casey's makeup, and it occurs to me that for someone who doesn't do kids, I've taken quite a shine to this sweet girl.

And what's not to love? She's smart and respectful and funny. Asher has done an amazing job with her.

They're both special. How could any woman have left them?

"Okay, you can look now."

"Oh!" she exclaims when she turns around. "I'm so pretty!"

"Yes you are."

"I haven't had this much fun since my mom died."

What?

I school my features, trying not to let her see that she's shocked the hell out of me. Her mom *died?*

She chooses some colors and goes to work on my face.

"I'm sorry that your mom passed away, sweetie."

"Yeah, it was a long time ago." I cringe when she chooses the blue eye shadow and begins brushing it on. She doesn't talk about her mom anymore, and I decide not to press her, but I do need to talk to Asher. How horrible for both of them.

When Casey is finishing up with me, the doorbell rings.

"That must be your uncle."

"Oh man," she whines and hops down from the counter. "Can't I just stay with you?"

"Your dad wants you to go hang out with your uncle."

I open the door to find a man that looks almost exactly like Asher in my doorway, with a beautiful woman at his side.

"Hi. I'm Mike."

"Lila." I shake his hand and invite them in.

"This is my wife, Fran."

"Why can't I stay with Lila?" Casey whines. "We are having a girls' day."

"Your daddy doesn't know how long he's going to be at work today," Fran says with a smile. "You look beautiful." She glances up at me. "I think Casey got the better end of this deal."

"She did good," I reply with a laugh. "Here, let's send a selfie to your dad."

I pull my phone out of my pocket, snap a photo of the two of us, and text it to Asher.

"We're going to go pack your bag, munchkin. You're gonna stay with us tonight," Fran says.

"Sleepover!" Casey exclaims. "You should come too, Lila!"

"I have work," I reply. "But maybe I'll see you again soon."

"Thanks for keeping her," Mike says with a grin. "Asher said he'll come over here when he's done. Lock your door." His face sobers and he pins me in a *I'm an authority figure and you'll do what I say* look.

"Let me guess, you're a cop too?"

"Guilty."

"I will lock the door. I will not let anyone in unless they have the password and know the secret handshake."

"You're a smart ass," Fran says with a smile. "I like you."

* * * *

I can't run. Why can't I run? I can hear someone coming for me, and it's dark, and I have to *run*, but my feet won't move. Heavy breathing is getting closer. I'm sweating, and trying to scream, but no sound comes out. Suddenly, it occurs to me that it's a dream. Wake up!

Banging on my front door finally rips me from the

nightmare. I sit up, my heart racing, eyes searching the room, and realize I must have fallen asleep on the couch.

"Lila!" More banging. I check my phone to find three missed texts and a missed call, all from Asher.

I pull the door open and am immediately tugged against him, his arms wrapped tightly around me and his face buried in my neck. He walks us inside and kicks the door closed, all without loosening his grip.

"Hey," I croon and hold on just as tight. He needs this. I can feel it. "Asher, are you okay?"

"I just need a minute." He takes a deep breath, and suddenly I'm in his arms and he's carrying me to the couch. He sits, with me in his lap, and continues to hold on tight.

"You're kind of scaring me," I whisper. My fingers brush through the soft, thick hair at the back of his head soothingly.

"I just want to hold you for a minute," he whispers. God, he's strong, and solid and...*safe*. His big hands rub up and down my back, as if he's reassuring himself that I'm here. His breathing is choppy. "We need to talk."

"Yes, we do." *We so do.*

"Are you okay?" He pushes me away, just far enough to look in my eyes. He brushes my hair away from my cheeks, his eyes worried.

"I'm fine."

"You didn't answer me. My texts or call."

"I fell asleep." I cup his face in my hands. "I just fell asleep."

He closes his eyes and takes a long, deep breath, and when he opens his eyes again, he's more in control now. "Was Casey okay? Did she give you any problems?"

"Casey is amazing," I reply truthfully and see his eyes soften with love and affection for his daughter. "I loved having her here."

He nods and holds on tight when I try to shift away, off of his lap.

"Stay here, please."

"Okay." I frown and watch him. His eyes are tired.

"Lila, there was another murder." He swallows hard.

"Who?" I whisper, not really wanting to hear the answer.

"Cheyenne."

"Oh." The tears come, falling down my cheeks unnoticed. "Oh, she was such a good kid."

"I know." He frowns and looks down, and I know he's not telling me everything.

"What else happened, Asher?"

"He's getting more violent, Lila. I'm not going to give you details because I can't, and because you don't need that living in your head."

Jesus, what did he do to her?

"Okay."

"And..."

He grows quiet again.

"And?"

He won't meet my gaze. Finally, he closes his eyes and swears under his breath, then looks up at me with eyes that are tormented and scared as hell.

"And what, Asher?"

"And you're a target."

"What?" I shake my head. "That doesn't make any sense. I'm not a student."

"What I'm about to tell you is confidential. This hasn't been released to the media." He brushes my hair over my shoulder tenderly. "With each victim, the killer has left a note. Threats. He talks about wanting revenge. But he's never specified a name before."

"But he did this time."

Asher nods and pulls a piece of paper out of his pocket, unfolds it, and shows it to me.

"This is a photocopy."

I read the note and feel my blood run cold.

"Oh my God."

I begin to shake and find myself caught up in Asher's arms again. He's rocking me now, holding me close. I can't get close enough.

"Why?" I whisper. "Asher, I don't understand. Oh my God! Those poor girls! They were all tortured and killed because of *me*?"

I pull out of his hold and stand, pacing the floor. I'm shaking. I can't breathe.

"This is my fault."

"Stop it, Lila. It's not your fault."

I whirl on him.

"He's after *me*." I shake my head wildly. "Who would do this?"

"Is there an ex out there somewhere that would want to hurt you?" He stands and takes my shoulders in his hands, rubs my arms firmly, trying to soothe me.

"I haven't dated since I've been here," I reply truthfully. "And I don't have any skeletons in my closet. I've had boyfriends, but those relationships ended on decent terms. There are no weirdos in my background, just guys that it didn't work out with."

"We are going to catch this guy," he promises me. He cups my face in his hands and looks deeply into my eyes. "I promise. Nothing is going to happen to you. I'm not going to lose you to this."

I hug him tightly and his words hit home. *I'm not going to lose you.*

"Speaking of losing someone." My voice is soft as I pull away. "Casey told me about her mom. I'm so sorry for your loss, Asher."

His lips firm, but he doesn't look sad or upset. He looks simply resigned.

"It's been four years," he says. "What did Casey tell you?"

"Just that she hadn't had that much fun since her mom

died."

He nods. "I was investigating another serial murderer in Seattle at the time. He was an evil bastard."

"Aren't they all?" I ask dryly.

"Yes." He brushes his fingertips down my cheek. He can't stop touching me. "He decided to play with the police, specifically the men who were trying to find him."

"No," I whisper.

"He killed her. It was staged to look like a car accident, but he confessed later to making that accident happen. Missy died instantly."

"Oh, Asher. I'm so sorry."

"How do you tell a six-year-old that her mama isn't coming home?" His voice is rough.

"How do you bury your young wife and raise your daughter alone?" The enormity of it hits me, and all I can think about is comforting him. Loving him.

I offer him my hand. "Come with me."

He follows me silently into my bedroom. I lead him onto the bed, over the covers, our clothes still on, and snuggle up to him, holding him close.

"Is this your way of comforting me?" he asks. His lips tip up into a half-smile.

"It's all I have," I reply with a shrug. It's more than I've ever offered to anyone else in my life.

I'm letting my walls down with this man, and as much as it scares me, I can't stop.

"I'm okay, baby. It's been a while. We've healed."

"Yes, but I just found out, and I'm hurting for you, Asher."

"God, you're sweet." He rolls me onto my back and kisses me softly, his hand resting on my jaw and neck. His lips are soft, sure. He teases me with his tongue as he eases his big body over mine and settles in to kiss the hell out of me.

It's pure heaven.

"Tell me I can stay," he whispers against my lips.

"What about the investigation?"

"We're done for the night."

"You can stay," I reply. He smiles and nibbles his way down my neck. His hands slip under my shirt and work it up over my head, then he discards my bra. "You're beautiful."

I smile shyly as he pulls a nipple into his mouth and lazily teases it, blows on it, then sucks some more. I tug his shirt up impatiently, getting caught up under his arms. His skin is warm and smooth over strong muscles.

"Can we take this off?" I ask. He sits up and in one fluid motion, pulls his shirt over his head and tosses it aside, then covers me again. He unfastens my jeans and slips his hand inside while his mouth travels down my torso, making me shimmy and squirm.

The things this man does with his mouth are *insane.*

His fingertips find my sweet spot and my hips surge up off the bed as electricity shoots through my body, sending fire along every nerve.

"God, you're so responsive. Do you know how long I've dreamed of your sweet little body?"

"Nine months," I pant with a smile. "Yes, I know exactly how long."

He chuckles and bites my stomach right next to my navel. "You've been in my dreams for months. I wake up aching for you."

Is it possible to come from words alone?

"Asher, I need you."

"I'm right here, baby."

"Need you inside me." I bury my fingers in his hair and hold on tight as his mouth continues the journey around my torso, along my ribs, under my breasts.

Who knew that the spot under my breasts was so fucking sensitive?

He's pulling my jeans down my legs, effortlessly, and kissing his way down to my hip.

"Trust me, I'm about to be inside you. God, you smell good."

"I don't wear perfume."

He grins up at me knowingly. Naughtily. God, I want to devour him.

"Not that kind of smell, Delila." He sniffs against my hip. "You smell like you want me to make love to you."

"I *so* want you to make love to me."

He growls as he makes quick work of sliding off his jeans, slips on protection, and covers me. He holds me tenderly, his forearms under my shoulders. His pelvis is cradled in mine, and he thrusts slowly back and forth, sliding his cock in my folds, hitting my clit each time.

"Oh my God," I whisper.

He kisses my lips as he pulls his hips back, and suddenly the tip is at my entrance, pushing inside. I'd forgotten how big he is.

"We'll take it easy," he assures me, watching me carefully. "God, you're so tight."

"Or you're big," I reply breathlessly, loving the way he feels as he eases inside me. "You feel so damn good."

"You're amazing." He stops when he's buried inside me completely and leans his forehead against mine. "So fucking amazing."

I clench around him and smile when he groans.

"God, don't do that."

I do it again.

"Lila, this won't last."

"We have all night, Lieutenant," I reply and clench again, circling my hips. "I'm right here. Let go."

His eyes shoot open, hot and intense, and he begins to move in long, steady, measured strokes, hitting every delicious nerve ending inside me, until I'm right there with him, ready to come out of my skin.

"Gonna come," I whisper.

"With me," he replies hoarsely. He grips my ass in one hand, tilting me up to meet him fully, and we come apart, crying out, clinging to each other.

"Amazing," he whispers and kisses my lips softly.

So fucking amazing.

* * * *

"Why aren't you sleeping?" he whispers against my ear, then kisses me there. He's spooned up behind me, his arms around me, holding me tight.

"Maybe I am," I reply with a grin.

"I can hear your wheels turning," he says and nudges me onto my back so he can see my face. He rests his hand on my belly and kisses my nose. "Talk to me."

"I'm—" I look to the ceiling, searching for my words.

"Sated? Impressed with my manliness? Ready to come again?"

"Confused," I reply with a sigh. "And impressed with your manliness."

"What are you confused about?"

I turn and hide my face in his chest, enjoying the way the light dusting of hair feels against my skin, but he cups my cheek in his hand and guides me back to look me in the eyes.

"What are you confused about, sweetheart?"

"How can I be this happy with you when there is a maniac out there killing my students, and he has some kind of crazy fixation on me? Does it make me a selfish person?"

"No."

"We're having sex—"

"Lila, it's not selfish. We're living our lives while we try to figure the rest of it out. We haven't forgotten it."

"I'm never going to forget it," I whisper.

"No," he agrees quietly and kisses my forehead. "You won't."

"How do you do this? Every day?" I hold on to him more tightly as I realize just how dangerous his job is. "*Why* do you do it?"

"I've always wanted to be a cop," he replies.

"But why homicide?"

"Someone has to stand for the dead, Lila." He kisses my forehead again, tenderly, but I can feel the energy pumping through him. "Someone has to stand over them and take care of them. To get that closure for their families. To make sure that the animal who killed them pays for it."

"But at what cost? Asher, what you see every day—"

"Makes me a better cop and a better man." He rolls away, onto his own back, and I follow him, bracing myself on his chest, watching him pull his thoughts together. "I've seen the worst of humanity there is, Lila. And I've seen the best."

"You are the best."

He tilts his head and searches my gaze for a long moment. "Thank you."

I shrug, suddenly embarrassed at speaking my thoughts out loud.

"Tell me something about you."

I blink at him. "What about me?"

"Tell me something about your childhood."

"You don't want to know about my childhood, Asher."

His eyes narrow. "Yes. I do."

I bite my lip and watch him quietly, but he doesn't insist. He just waits. And here, in the dark and in the quiet of this honest moment, I trust him.

"I didn't know my mom." His gaze snaps to mine in surprise.

"You were raised by your dad?"

I smirk. "If you can call it that. Mom left before I could crawl. I was a mistake and she didn't want me." Asher reaches up to tuck my hair behind my ear, but I flinch away.

I don't want him to touch me while I tell him this.

"Dad was an alcoholic and enjoyed the occasional recreational drug."

"Lila—"

"It could have been worse. And there were long stretches of time when he'd sober up and things would be relatively normal for a while. But inevitably, he'd fall off the bandwagon and I'd be left to fend for myself."

"You should be so proud of yourself," he says softly.

"I am," I agree. "My life could have gone very badly had I not had Kate in my life, and a fierce stubbornness. I made my mind up early on that I wouldn't end up like my father."

"You're amazing," he says.

"I'm strong," I reply.

"Okay, so back to the original statement. What are you confused about? Because I don't think you're confused about the sex we just had in light of the circumstances."

"You've made me rethink things that I thought I believed," I admit softly.

"Such as?"

I shake my head and am embarrassed to feel my eyes fill with tears.

"What is it, baby?"

"I've been very good at keeping my heart safe, Asher. I don't long for children, because I don't think that I'd be a good parent given what I come from. I don't have one-night stands, but I also don't think about being with anyone for the long term."

His eyes flare, but he stays quiet, waiting for me to finish.

"But—" I swallow hard.

"But?"

"I enjoy you. I enjoy Casey."

"We enjoy you too."

I nod, ridiculously happy to hear those words.

"So, we'll just enjoy each other," he adds with an encouraging smile. "And see where it goes from there."

He pulls me back into his arms and kisses my cheek, then my lips.

"We'll just see where it goes," I whisper, liking the sound of that but knowing that I'm quickly losing my heart to this amazing man and his daughter.

Chapter Six

~Asher~

"Wake up, sleepy head." I climb onto the bed, steaming mug of coffee in hand, and lean over to kiss Lila's forehead. I can't seem to keep my hands—or my lips—off of her. And she doesn't seem to mind.

"Want to," she mumbles and frowns, her eyes still closed.

"Come on, Delila, wake up."

She sniffs the air. "Do I smell coffee?"

"Yes." I grin and climb off the bed, then saunter naked toward the bathroom. "It'll be in the bathroom with me."

"I don't want it that bad!" she calls out.

Okay, so she's not a morning person. She can't be perfect.

"I'm naked," I reply. "You have twenty seconds to get your sweet ass in the shower with me before I come haul you in myself."

"Whatever, caveman," I hear her mumble, and my heart stumbles with the immediate love I feel for her.

I haven't felt this in…four years.

I recognize it. I'm in love with her. How it managed to happen so fast, I don't know. And while I do recognize it, it feels different this time. Not better or worse, just different.

Because she's not Missy. She's Lila. I'm not replacing what I had, I'm adding to what I have now, and that feels pretty fucking good.

I start the water, set a condom inside the shower because I want to take her there this morning, sip the coffee, and grin when I feel her move up behind me, press her spectacular naked body against my back and a kiss to my shoulder.

"Good morning," she whispers sweetly.

"Good morning."

"May I please have some coffee now?"

I snort. "You don't have to put on the sweet act, darlin'. I'll share my coffee."

"Thank God," she says and takes the mug out of my hand, then downs it in three big gulps.

"Uh, that was hot."

"Thank God," she repeats with a grin and steps into the shower. "So is this!" Her voice is a high-pitched shriek.

"Do not turn it down," I order her and step in with her.

"Are you trying to burn me?"

"You'll drink boiling hot coffee but you won't shower in hot water?"

"This isn't hot. This is..." She flails her hands about. "This is *really* hot."

"Brain not working yet?" I kiss her forehead and laugh when she pinches my ass. She's smiling, her eyes shining and happy, still a little sleepy, and her skin is still warm from bed and soft, and I can't stand it.

I need her.

Now.

I lift her and brace her against the wall of the shower, making her cry out at the cold against her back.

"What the hell?"

"Need you," I murmur against her sweet mouth. I hold the condom up to her lips, and she grips the wrapper in her teeth, helping me rip it open. I roll it on, then boost her up and slide inside her, and nothing has ever felt so fucking good in all my life. "Do you know how damn good you feel?"

"If it's anything like how you feel, it's pretty damn good," she replies and bites my lip. "Didn't we do this just a few hours ago?"

"We made love a few hours ago," I reply and hold on to her ass in the palm of my hands, just this side of too rough. She gasps and bites her lip. "That was life-affirming sex."

"What's this?" she asks and gasps again as I begin to move hard and fast, chasing both of our orgasms.

"This is good, old-fashioned fucking," I growl against her neck. "I want you hard and fast, right here in the shower."

"You're getting it," she replies and leans in to bite my shoulder as she comes hard, her legs gripping on to my hips like vices, grinding her pelvis against my own. "Christ, Asher."

"That's right," I murmur and feel myself go blind as my balls lift and tighten with my own release. "Just me."

"Just you."

* * * *

"I'm going to need you to pack a bag," I inform Lila as I tug my shirt over my head and finger-comb my hair. She's already dressed, looking sexy as fuck in a red sundress that I want to peel off her.

God, I'm out of control.

"Why?" she asks with a frown.

"Because you're going to come stay with me until we catch this fucker."

She slides her feet into black flip-flops, then props her hands on her lean hips, and I know I'm in for an argument.

"No, I'm not."

"Yes. You are."

She narrows her eyes at me. God, she's magnificent when she's pissed.

"You know, I'm happy to take precautions, and you can boss me around all you want in the bedroom—"

"Like that, do you?"

"But you *will not* tell me where I'm going to live."

"Look, Lila."

"No, *you* look." She's pacing now, really worked up, and it's a sight to behold. "I've worked long and hard for my independence. I'm not a stupid woman."

"Didn't say you are."

"And I know how to look out for myself! I've been doing it since I was a kid. I didn't have a mom, Asher. My dad was drunk most of the time. I've held jobs and taken care of myself since before I could do algebra."

"I still can't do algebra," I reply, trying to keep it light, but my hands are in fists now at the thought of a young Lila taking care of herself. Her father should have his face beat in.

"I'm not going to be your pawn, that just does as you say. I'm not one of your officers."

"No, you're not." I pull her to me now, drawing her into my arms, and hug her tight. She melts into these hugs like she doesn't get them often, and that just softens me toward her even more. "You're not my pawn, Lila. You're *everything*."

"Excuse me?" she whispers, not looking up.

"I don't know if you've been paying attention, baby, but this isn't a quick fuck for me. You're not just a job for me."

"What am I?"

I swallow hard and kiss her head. "You mean more to me than any woman has in a very long time. Let me protect you. I can't just pack up my daughter and move in with you. If it was just me, I would. I need you to come to me."

"That's the other thing." She pushes out of my arms and stomps away. "Casey."

I still and my heart stops. "Are you saying you have a problem with my daughter?"

"No!" She whirls around, eyes wide, and I immediately calm. "I adore her. Asher, I can't bring whatever this could be to your house. I would *die* before I put Casey in danger!"

"*You're* in danger here, Delila. No one is in danger at my

house. The killer has no reason to know that you'll be with me. I don't like knowing that you're miles away from me. I can't get here in time if something were to happen."

I pace away and push my hands through my hair, suddenly frustrated.

"Damn it, Lila, I need you with me."

"Casey—"

"Will be fine." I turn back to her. "Do you honestly think that I'd willingly put my daughter in danger? She's safe, just like you will be if you come with me."

She chews on her lip, giving it some thought, and if I wasn't already completely in love with her, her concern for Casey would have pushed me right over.

"Okay," she says cautiously. "But when you're not home, Casey should stay with Mike and Fran."

I frown, but she continues before I can say anything.

"Not because I don't love spending time with her, but because *no one* would follow her to Mike's house. If you're not home to protect her, she shouldn't be alone with me. Just in case."

I cup her face in my hands and everything in me is screaming to tell her I love her.

"Thank you," I say instead.

"You won't be thanking me when I use up all the hot water and burn toast."

I grin. "I already burn the toast."

Chapter Seven

~Lila~

It's been two weeks since Cheyenne was killed. Two weeks without so much as a leaf blowing the wrong way in the trees. Spring has bloomed in New Orleans, making the city seem fresh and bright.

I've attended four funerals in the last month, and the sadness of the loss of the girls hangs heavily around me, despite the brightness of early summer. The killer has been quiet—too quiet—and I can't help but worry that something could happen at any moment.

Classes are out for the weekend, and Asher's friends, Matt and Nic, from Seattle are coming to visit for a few days. In fact, their plane should have landed not long ago. They're going to meet us at home.

I mean, Asher's townhouse.

Except, it's come to feel like home over the past two weeks. Most of my clothes have managed to migrate there, much to Casey's delight. She thinks it's awesome that every night is a sleepover, and she's loved getting to know Kate and Eli, who have been invited over for dinner several times.

I've refused the four hundred and twenty-three offers to sleep in his bed from Asher. I don't feel comfortable sleeping with him with Casey there. I don't want to confuse her.

Hell, *I'm* confused enough for both of us.

That doesn't mean that he doesn't sneak into the spare bedroom with me after she goes to sleep. There have been a few times that he's carried me into his bed to make love to me because he wants to have me there.

Jesus, I'm in love with him. With both of them.

Who knew?

"Lila!"

I spin on the sidewalk to find Colin and Stacy, both from my US Women's History class, running toward me.

"Hi, guys. What's up?"

"We wanted to see if you've graded our essays yet."

I grin at them and shake my head. "I'm sorry, not yet. I'm going to grade them over the weekend."

"Do you ever take a day off?" Colin asks with the shake of his head. He's just about my height, dressed casually in jeans and a plain white T-shirt.

Stacy, his roommate and best friend, is a plump girl with curly blonde hair and big brown eyes. They're holding hands, as they always do.

College kids seem to be very affectionate with each other.

"Once in a while," I reply with a laugh. "What are you guys up to?"

"I have a date tonight," Colin says and wiggles his eyebrows. "New guy I met the other day at Starbucks."

"I want to meet this guy," Stacy says and pokes Colin in the ribs. "He's probably not good enough for you."

"They never are, darling," Colin replies and kisses Stacy on the cheek. "Do you have fun plans this weekend, Lila?"

"Yes, actually. I have friends coming in from out of town."

"Awesome." Stacy grins and checks her watch. "Oh, hell. I have to go pick my baby sister up from school. Give me a ride, Colin?"

"You guys stick close together," I add sternly. "I want you to stay safe."

Colin's eyes grow sad. "If I'd stayed with Cheyenne longer,

she wouldn't have—"

"You don't know that," Stacy says and kisses his cheek. "It's not your fault. The police even told you so."

His eyes narrow a bit at the reminder of being interrogated after Cheyenne's death.

"She's right," I reassure him. "You couldn't have known what would happen after you took her home. But be safe out there, you guys."

"Sure. See you next week, Lila."

"Bye guys." I wave, get in the car, and take off toward home.

I mean, Asher's townhouse, damn it.

When I pull into the driveway, I see a strange car parked behind Asher. They beat me here.

"You brought me strawberry cupcakes!" Casey exclaims as I walk through the front door. She launches herself into a petite brunette's arms, hugging her tight. "I missed you so much, Nic!"

"I missed you too," Nic replies and hugs her back, then catches my eye. "You must be Lila."

"Guilty," I reply with a smile. "And you're Nic."

"She makes the best cupcakes in the whole world," Casey informs me and bites into a pink cupcake.

"I've heard," I reply with a laugh.

"I brought about two dozen, all different kinds." Nic shakes my hand, then simply pulls me into a hug. "It's so nice to meet you."

"You too."

"Hey, baby," Asher says as he and a tall man—a tall, impossibly handsome man—walk into the room. Asher plants a firm kiss on me and looks into my eyes. "You okay?"

"Great." I smile at Matt. "I'm Lila."

"Matt." He shakes my hand and pulls me away from Asher and into his arms, hugging me tight. "And you're gorgeous. Why are you with that asshole? Sorry, Casey."

"It's okay," she says without looking up from her cupcake.

"You might want to stop touching her," Asher says with mutiny in his eyes, only making Matt hug me tighter.

"Ignore him," Nic says with a laugh. "You know how he loves to piss you off."

"He's good at it."

I pull out of Matt's hug and reach for a cupcake. Chocolate deliciousness explodes in my mouth.

"Marry me." I turn to Nic. "Divorce him and marry me. I don't leave the toilet seat up, and I totally understand PMS."

She laughs and shakes her head. "Sorry. I'm all his. But I can ship cupcakes down here whenever you want."

"I love you," I tell her earnestly as I lick frosting off my fingers. I glance up at Asher in time to see a strange look cross his face, but then he seems to catch himself and grins.

"We all love Nic. I tried to talk her into marrying me at least a dozen times before they got married."

"My loss," Nic says with a shrug and a smile, then melts into her husband's side when he wraps his arm around her shoulders. He leans in and whispers something in her ear, making Nic blush. "Not here," she whispers to him.

"Newlyweds," Asher says just as the doorbell rings.

"That's Masie!" Casey exclaims and runs for the door. "We're having a sleepover!"

"Wait!" Asher and Matt both yell at the same time, bringing Casey up short.

"You don't just open the door, Casey. We've discussed this," Asher says as he stomps toward the door.

"But it's just Masie," Casey says.

"You don't know that," Asher replies.

"Things still intense down here?" Nic asks.

"Not really." I shrug and snatch up another cupcake. Strawberry this time. "Things have been quiet for a few weeks now. It's weird." I bite into the cake and immediately know what all the fuss is about. It's absolutely delicious. "Seriously, you should make these for a living."

Nic laughs. "You're right, I should."

I wink at her, perfectly aware that Nic owns a successful cupcake bakery in Seattle. Asher loves his friends and has told me all about them. He and Matt were partners for nearly ten years.

"Well, Casey is off for her sleepover," Asher says as he rejoins us in the kitchen. "She'll be back tomorrow morning. She wants to go on the cemetery tour with us."

"Fun," I reply. "I haven't done the cemetery tour yet."

"How long have you lived here?" Matt asks as he lays his hand on the back of Nic's neck, massaging gently, as if she belongs to him and touching her is second nature to him.

It's sexy as hell.

"Since last fall," I reply and swallow the last of my cupcake. "But I jumped right into work and haven't taken the time to explore the city. So, thanks for letting me tag along this weekend."

"You're not tagging along," Asher says and kisses my cheek. "Not coming isn't an option."

"Oh right," I reply and frown. "Because you're keeping tabs on me."

"No, because I don't want to be without you," he whispers in my ear. "Keeping tabs on you is the excuse I use."

I roll my eyes, but I'm lit up inside. When he says things like that, I can't help but swoon.

"What are we doing this evening?" Nic asks. "I'm hungry."

"Are you okay?" Matt immediately asks her, concerned.

"I'm fine." Nic turns to me. "Don't mind him. He freaks out when I talk about food. I'm diabetic."

"Punishments happen when you make light of it," he says calmly, as if he's reminding her, and my eyebrows climb into my hairline.

"Excuse me?"

"It's okay," Nic assures me. "These are punishments that I

like."

I glance at Asher, who just coughs into his fist and pretends *not* to say, "Pervert," making us all laugh.

"Okay then." I glance around, clearly missing the joke. "Well, it's about dinner time anyway. Why don't we head into the French Quarter to eat?"

"Perfect," Nic says. I nod my head in agreement and remember that I was supposed to stop by my apartment after class to change into a cute sundress and matching bra and panties I'd bought about a month ago, just in case I ever started to date again.

This counts.

"Why don't you guys go ahead?" I cover the cupcakes and set them aside before I devour the rest. "I will meet you. I have to swing by my apartment."

"No." Asher frowns and crosses his arms over his chest. "No way."

"You're being silly." I roll my eyes. "I'll be there in just a little bit."

"There's a killer out there," Asher reminds me. "No."

"I'll ride with her," Nic offers with a smile. "We'll have girl time that way. You can drive Matt into the French Quarter, get us a table, have a beer, and we'll be right behind you."

Asher shakes his head, but I lay my hand on his arm. "Asher. Nothing has happened in *weeks*. We'll be fine."

"What do you need at your apartment?"

I grin and bat my eyelashes. "Casey isn't coming home tonight. That means I get to sleep with you all night. And I might have something pretty to show you."

His face softens, and he cups my jaw in his hand, then leans in and presses his lips to mine. "Okay. Please be careful."

"Don't you know? Careful is my middle name."

* * * *

"So," Nic begins about five minutes away from the townhouse. "Tell me about Asher."

"Well, he has dark hair, gorgeous eyes. He's tall, not quite as tall as Matt. His arms are To. Die. For. Seriously, he's got muscles on his arms *for days*."

Nic laughs.

"Okay, tell me about *you* and Asher."

I glance at her, to find her smiling at me. "Well, I'm completely in love with him."

"Duh."

I blink and change lanes.

"That obvious, huh?"

"Oh yeah." Nic nods. "What do you love about him?"

"His arms," I reply immediately and then sober as a flood of responses fill my head. "The way he holds me. His arms are hot, but they're also strong and when he holds me, it's the safest I've ever felt." I turn down my street. "His laugh. Sharing his coffee with me in the morning. The way he touches my face when he kisses me. How much he loves his daughter, and how he parents her."

"That's a lot."

"And it's only the beginning," I reply honestly. "There's so much to love about him." I pull to a stop, put the car in park, and turn to my new friend.

"You're right." Nic smiles reassuringly. "There is a lot to love about him, and I'm very glad that you see that. How did you meet?"

"On an airplane last summer." I grin, cut the engine, and turn to look at Nic. "I fell in his lap."

"In his lap?" She giggles. "Do tell."

"Well, we had arrived here, and I was standing, trying to get my bag from the overhead compartment, and this man pushed me, sending me right into Asher's lap." I worry my bottom lip between my teeth. "I noticed his arms then, too. He laughed, planted his hands on my hips, and helped me up."

"Hot," Nic says and waves her hand over her face.

"So hot," I agree. "Was that a test?"

"Of course."

"Did I pass?"

"With flying colors. You're good for him. I see changes in him, all for the better. His eyes aren't sad anymore." Her own eyes fill with tears as she thinks. "And when he looks at you, he lights up. It's beautiful, and I'm happy for both of you."

"Thank you." Her words have lit *me* up inside. "I'll be back in a few."

"I'll be here," she says and pulls her phone out of her bag. "I'll just text my sister-in-law, Brynna, and let her know we arrived safely."

"Great." I jog up the steps to my apartment and let myself in. It's strange to be here. It almost doesn't feel like mine anymore. It smells musty, the way a place does when you've been on an extended vacation.

I walk back to the bedroom, grab the dress and underwear from my closet, and am about to change when I hear footsteps behind me.

"You can make yourself at home. I wouldn't want to wait in the car either. It's hot out there. I'll be right out."

"Hello, Lila."

I spin, shocked that it isn't Nic that's let herself into my apartment, but Colin from class.

"Colin? What are you doing in here?"

"Oh, you didn't hear me knock? I'm sorry." He looks nervous and apologetic, so I smile reassuringly.

"It's okay, but what can I help you with? I'm on my way out."

"Oh, I just have a couple questions about class."

I frown at him, alarm bells going off like crazy. "You can ask me all the questions you want on Monday. I'd like for you to leave, please."

His face transforms from apologetic and nervous to

simply…evil. A slow grin spreads over his face. His eyes grow cold.

"I'm not leaving, Lila."

"What the hell is this, Colin?"

"Don't you remember?" He's circling me now, cracking his knuckles almost absentmindedly. "I have a date tonight."

"Yes, with the guy from Starbucks."

He nods, that creepy smile still on his face. "No. With you."

My heart kicks up into overtime, and a cold sweat breaks out over my skin. *Colin is the killer!*

"Colin, I don't know what you want, but I'm quite sure we can talk about this."

"Oh, we're going to talk about it. We're going to do a lot of talking, actually." He's advancing on me. My mind is racing, trying to figure out how to get past him, out of this room and outside. "You're going to get really tired of talking. And then I'm going to cut your tongue out of your pretty little mouth."

"What?" I can't breathe. I can't think. "I'm not going anywhere with you, Colin. And my boyfriend knows where I am."

He laughs, the sound of it raking down my spine, making me want to throw up.

"You don't have to go willingly, Lila." I try to run, but he grabs my arm, yanks me against him, and hits me on the head with something hard, making me black out cold.

Chapter Eight

~Asher~

"So, things are going well with Lila." Matt sips his soda and watches me across the table of the crowded restaurant. I check my watch for the fifteenth time. The girls should be here by now.

"They are." I smirk. "Are we going to get all girlie and talk about our feelings now?"

"I like her," he says. "She's good for you."

She's fucking amazing.

"Am I supposed to feel guilty, man?" I ask and glance out the window to the busy French Quarter.

"For what?"

"For moving on. For falling in love again. I loved Missy, you know I did. And it killed me when she died." If it weren't for Casey, I don't know how I would have survived losing her.

"Missy would be pissed that you're even thinking about feeling guilty," Matt replies. "Asher, *you* didn't die. It's okay to move on and live your life."

"Missy would be pissed," I agree with a laugh.

"What does Casey think of her?"

My heart softens as I think of how great Lila is with my daughter. "She loves her. They have a good time together. And Lila is so patient with her. And she *listens*, you know? She doesn't brush Casey off."

"I'm happy for you, friend."

"Yeah, thanks. How is the family?"

"They're all crazy," Matt replies with a laugh. "There are so many of us now, when we get together it's absolute chaos."

"And you wouldn't have it any other way," I reply dryly.

Matt's phone rings. "Hey, little one. Are you on your way?"

He frowns, catches my eye, then puts the call on speaker and sets the phone on the table. "Okay, you're on speaker. What's going on?"

"Lila was gone longer than I thought she would be," Nic says, her voice shaky, and my entire body goes cold. "I went up to see what the hold up was, and she's not here."

"What do you mean *she's not there?*" I ask, immediately throwing bills on the table for our drinks and heading for the door.

"She's gone. Her door was wide open and she's not here."

"Don't touch anything, Nic," Matt says, right behind me, racing to the car. "We're on our way. Go back to the car and lock the doors."

"I'm sorry," she says with tears in her voice.

"It's going to be okay," Matt assures her as I start the car and speed into traffic, headed to Lila's. I pull my own phone out and call Jordan.

"Hello."

"He's got Lila." My heart stops, saying the words out loud. "He took her from her apartment. I'm on my way there now."

"I'll be there in ten."

She hangs up and I immediately call dispatch. "This is Lieutenant Asher Smith. I have a possible abduction, connected to an ongoing case, at 4268 Tulane Avenue. I need all available units to respond."

"Copy that, Lieutenant," Dispatch responds. "Sending all available units."

I hang up and swear ripely.

"We're going to find her," Matt says calmly, but his hands are in fists. I know he's as worried as I am. "Walk me through it."

I spend the ten minutes to Lila's apartment filling Matt in on the specifics of the case. Fuck protocol.

Lila's life is at stake.

I pull into the parking lot, next to Lila's car. Nic rushes to Matt and hugs him tightly.

"I'm so sorry. She was gone for like twenty minutes, and I thought I should check. I should have gone in with her."

"No, then we might be looking for both of you." Matt holds her face and looks her in the eyes intently. "I want you to take Lila's car and go to Asher's."

"I should stay and help—"

"That was not a question, Nicole." Matt's voice is hard. "I want you out of here."

"My address is in the GPS," I tell her as I run past and up the stairs to Lila's apartment. The door is still standing open. I search each room, praying that Nic's wrong and she really is here, but the rooms are empty.

"When was she taken?" Jordan asks as she runs into the apartment, Matt right behind her, and I'm shocked to see my brother bring up the rear.

"Less than thirty minutes," I reply. "Thanks for coming, Mike."

"I heard the call come in. I wasn't far away. What do we know?"

"Jack shit," I reply with frustration and pace the room. "We know he took her."

"Do we know that for sure?" Jordan asks.

"She wouldn't just leave. Yes, he took her."

My phone rings in my pocket, and I pray it's Lila, but it's Kate's office number, Lila's best friend. I send it to voice mail and shove my fingers through my hair.

"Uniforms are pulling in," Mike says as he looks outside.

"Send them out on foot patrol," I instruct him. "I want this entire neighborhood canvassed."

"He might have taken her in a car."

I frown, fighting to think clearly. "I doubt it. Nic would have seen Lila being dragged to a car in the parking lot. Lila would have screamed."

"Not if he took her out the back," Matt replies grimly. "They could be anywhere by now."

My phone rings again. Kate. This time I accept the call. "Kate, I don't have time to talk."

"Lila's on my cell phone." Her voice is scared. "I can't hear everything that's happening, but she keeps saying *Colin*. She sounds scared. What is happening?"

"Colin?" I ask and search wildly for Jordan. "Is she still on the line?"

"Yes."

"*Do not hang up*, do you hear me?" I put Kate on speaker. "Put it on speaker and hold it up to your phone."

"Okay, but you can't hear much. What's happening, Asher?"

"Lila's in trouble, and you're going to help me find her, sweetheart."

"I'm calling in to get a trace on Lila's cell," Jordan says, her phone already to her ear.

"Please, Colin, you don't have to do this."

My gut seizes at Lila's scared voice, but I'm so relieved to hear that she's still alive.

"Kate, put your cell on mute. I don't want any noises to go through Lila's phone. I don't want Colin to hear us."

"I already did that," Kate says. "I did it as soon as I realized Lila was in trouble."

"Good girl," Matt says. "And who the fuck is Colin?"

"It has to be Colin Forester, from her history class," Jordan says then speaks back into her phone. "Yes, I need a trace on 504-555-3297, now. There's a live call on it right now."

"Talk to me about Colin," Matt says.

I rack my brain, trying to picture the boy. "He's in her class and the study group. Roughly five foot six, bald. He had solid alibis for every murder."

"He escorted Cheyenne home the night she was killed," Jordan adds.

"And had an alibi ten minutes later," I remind her.

"His roommate said she heard him come home. But could she be covering for him?" Jordan speaks into her phone again, barking instructions for the trace on Lila's phone.

"Bald?" Matt asks with a frown. "Like, he might have a full head of hair if he let it grow?"

"Yes." My eyes narrow. "Son of a bitch. He shaves so he doesn't leave evidence. Where is that trace?"

"They're working on it," Jordan says.

"No, please don't," Lila says through my phone.

"Asher, he's going to hurt her," Kate says urgently. "He just said something about her fingers."

Jordan and I lock gazes. "He has a thing for cutting off his victims fingers."

"Motherfucker," Mike mutters.

"Get an address for Colin," I tell my brother.

"No need, we have a trace," Jordan says, her eyes confused.

"Where is she?"

"Asher, she's *here.*"

"Clearly she's not," I reply angrily. "What the fuck?"

"The address is here."

"She's in another apartment," Matt says.

"Fan out," I order and head for the door. "Break down every fucking door in this complex."

Chapter Nine

~Lila~

"Wake up, Lila."

My head is screaming.

"Come on, I didn't hit you that hard. Don't be a pussy or this won't be any fun."

"I need to throw up."

"Fine. There's a bucket next to you." He sighs, as if he's horribly disappointed in me. "I really thought you'd be a better sport than this."

I reach for it and lose my lunch, then open my eyes and take in my surroundings. I'm on a couch in an apartment that looks very much like mine. Colin from my class is sitting in a chair across the room from me.

"I'm not tied up?" I ask inanely. Jesus, I've been kidnapped, and all I can think to say is *I'm not tied up?*

"If you try to run, I'll simply kill you," he replies calmly. His face, his body, everything about him is perfectly steady, as though he does this every day. "Tying you up would take some of the fun out of what I have planned."

He stands and begins to pace the room. I glance over to the front door to see that it's locked with a padlock. No escaping that way.

Colin is rattling around in the kitchen, and I take this opportunity to pat my pockets, praying for my phone, and find it. I have time to dial the last number I called, lock it, and stuff it back in my pocket before he comes back in the room.

Please, Kate, pick up.

"Now that you're awake, I'll start setting up." He smiles happily, even joyfully, and begins laying syringes and different medical instruments on the coffee table. "We can chat while I work."

"Why are you doing this?"

"Well, it's easier to have these things on hand so I don't have to go back and forth to the kitchen." He laughs at his own joke, having a great time, and I just feel like I have to throw up again.

God, how am I going to get out of this?

"Colin, I like you."

"Do you?" He smiles, then all expression leaves his face. "Is that why you flunked me out of your class last semester?"

"You failing the class had nothing to do with whether I like you."

"I didn't fail!" he yells angrily. "*You* flunked me!"

I swallow hard as I watch him reign in his temper.

"I've never failed a class before, you know." He begins laying tools out again, perfectly calm. "I am in pre-med. I don't fail classes. I had to pay for that fucking class *twice*."

"Really? All of this because you failed a class?"

"I DON'T FAIL CLASSES!"

"Why did you hurt those girls?" I ask, trying to distract him by changing the subject.

"Because I was trying to scare you." He smiles smugly. "And it worked. Eventually. At first you didn't seem very scared, so I just made more of a mess and got your attention."

"You tortured them?"

"Of course." He shrugs, like it's no big deal. "Well, I didn't torment the first one the way I wanted to. I was nervous with her. So, I fucked her, then I beat her until she died."

I swallow hard, wanting to throw up again. Jesus, what those girls went through, all because of *me*.

"But, hey, live and learn, you know?" He winks. "It was so easy to fool all of you. Did you seriously think I was gay?"

"I didn't really pay attention."

"Sure you did." He sits back on his heels and tips his head to the side. "I told you I had a date with a boy."

"Okay."

"Now you're just trying to hurt my feelings. I know you've been paying attention to me." He shakes his finger at me. "You're a naughty girl."

"Colin, you don't have to do this."

"I begged you not to fail me."

"I asked you to come to study group so I could help you," I remind him, stalling for time.

"Your study group is a fucking joke," he replies. "But, I found some fun playmates that way. That last one? Cheyenne? What a cock tease."

"She was your friend." *And sweet, and young.*

"She led me on," he replies sharply. "She wanted me."

I take a deep breath, praying that Kate has heard this and called Asher. Where is Asher? What if this maniac kills me and I never get to tell Asher that I love him?

What about Casey?

Tears fill my eyes, making Colin laugh. "Tears don't work on me, Lila. All of the others cried too."

"Are you going to rape me, Colin?"

"Of course." He shakes his head like I'm an idiot. "Did you get my notes? I'm surprised you didn't know this was coming. I sent notes for you."

"With the victims."

He simply raises a brow.

"I saw the last one."

"See, that's where I fucked up." He sighs dejectedly. "I

should have sent them to you directly and not left them with the girls. But, I thought it was more dramatic that way. It didn't occur to me that the cops wouldn't show them to you."

"Is that why you named me specifically in the last one?"

"Yeah. But then you had to spread your legs for that fucking cop and he took you away." He glares at me. "God, you're such a whore. What was the purpose of moving into your building, knowing your schedule better than my own, if that dick was just going to suddenly decide to protect you and take you away?"

He's been living in my building?

"I thought you lived with Stacy."

"I rented this place under my mom's name." He smiles, proud of himself again. "I come and go as I please, and watch you. Well, I watched you until that fucker of a cop moved you in with him. You must be an amazing fuck." He grins. "I'll find out for myself soon enough."

"He's going to come looking for me, Colin." Bile has risen in the back of my throat.

"True. So we better get started." He claps his hands gleefully and reaches for a syringe. "I planned this all perfectly. I didn't leave even *one* clue for the cops. Why do you think I shave my head? I shave my whole fucking body so I never leave any hair behind. No DNA. No prints."

"So you're just going to murder me in *your apartment?*" I ask calmly. "You'll get caught."

"I'll claim I found you." He shrugs carelessly. "Everyone thinks I'm weak and sweet. They'll overlook me."

He comes at me with the syringe.

"What is that?"

"Oh, don't worry. It won't kill you. It'll just make you really groggy so I can have fun with you without you fighting me."

"Colin, please." I try to scramble away, but he sticks the needle in my arm and shoots it into my body.

"See? Otherwise you'll fight me." He smiles and walks

away. "Don't worry, it'll make you sleepy, but I'll keep you awake." He grabs hedge trimmers and inspects them. "I think that after I fuck you, I'll take your fingers off first."

Jesus, I'm going to be sick. I'm sweaty now, panting, and already starting to feel fuzzy.

"Please don't do this," I whisper and feel myself start to slip into sleep, but suddenly Colin slaps me across the face.

"No sleeping," he says harshly. "You're gonna want to feel me inside you, Lila. I'm fucking amazing."

"No."

He lifts my dress, knocking my phone out of my pocket and onto the floor, face down, thank God.

"You won't need that anyway."

He reaches for my panties. My arms are heavy. Everything is heavy. I can't fight him off. Suddenly, the door is knocked open with a crash and Matt rushes in, yelling, "In here!" as he attacks Colin, pulling him off of me and punching him in the jaw.

"You can't hit him," Jordan says from the doorway.

God, I'm sleepy. My eyes close, but I try to stay awake to hear what's happening.

They saved me!

"I'm not on the job," Matt says calmly and I hear him hit Colin again.

"Baby?"

Asher!

"Baby, wake up." His hands are on my face and I fight to open my eyes. He looks scared. "Lila, stay with me."

"Can't stay awake."

"What did you give her?" Matt asks, but I don't hear Colin respond.

"Gotta sleep."

"I need an ambulance—" I hear Jordan's voice call for the ambulance, and I can feel Asher's amazing hands slip under me and lift me against him. God, I love his arms. There is nothing better than being in his arms.

"Love you," I whisper into his neck.

"God, I love you too, baby. You're going to be okay."

I smile, relieved, and I can't fight it anymore. I'm so heavy.

* * * *

"Open those gorgeous eyes, baby."

My head hurts. I can't move. It feels like I'm moving through water. What happened? Was I in an accident?

And then it all comes crashing back. Colin, knocking me out, evil, telling me about the girls.

He's going to kill me!

I lash out, struggling to move, but when I open my eyes, it's Asher holding me, his mouth grim and eyes hard.

"Asher?"

"You're safe, Lila. You're okay. Shhh."

The tears come fast and hard and I collapse against him as he joins me on the hospital bed, holding me tight, crooning to me as I cry out the fear.

"I was so scared," I whisper.

"About ten years have been taken off my life today," he agrees and plants his lips on my head. "You're so fucking smart, Lila. Calling Kate was genius."

"It worked?"

"Perfectly. She called me and we traced your phone. That's how we found you."

"Thank God." I hold onto him tightly. "Colin?"

"In custody, bragging about his victims. He's going away for a very long time."

I nod, suddenly sad for him too. "He's just a kid."

"He's a fucking murderer, Lila."

"I know." I frown and pull back so I can see Asher's face. "Thank you, for finding me. For rescuing me."

"I will always find you," he replies and wipes my tears away with his thumbs. "God, Lila, I was so afraid that I wouldn't find you in time. It was the most helpless, worthless feeling in the world. You've become one of the two most important people in my life. I can't lose you."

"I'm right here." I grip on to his wrists. "Asher, I love you. I was so sad that I might not get to tell you that. I know it happened fast, and it seems crazy, but I am so in love with you and Casey both, and the thought of not having you in my life is...*devastating*."

"Ah sweetheart." He kisses my forehead, then my lips. "I love you."

"Can I come in?" Casey asks from the doorway.

"Of course." I grin at the sweet girl as she walks to the bed and climbs right up with me, as if it's the most natural thing in the world.

"Are you okay?" she asks with wide, worried eyes.

"I'm still a little groggy, but I'm doing much better."

"Daddy was scared," she whispers to me and I feel Asher grin beside me.

"I was scared too," I reply and brush her pretty red hair over her shoulder. "But I'm fine."

"Okay." She suddenly frowns. "When can you come home?"

I blink rapidly at the question. *Home.* But the townhouse that Asher and Casey share isn't my home.

"In a few hours," Asher replies. "As soon as the stuff making her tired is out of her body."

"You can take me to my apartment," I say softly, secretly scared to death of staying even one minute in that place alone.

"Why?" he asks, sincerely puzzled.

"It's my home."

"No it isn't," Casey interrupts.

I simply look between both of these people that I've come to love so much. Asher takes my hand and kisses my knuckles.

"Home is where we are, Lila."

I feel tears fill my eyes and try to blink them away.

"Don't you want to stay with us?" Casey asks.

"Of course," I reply and kiss her cheek. "Of course I do."

"But you're not staying in the spare bedroom anymore," Asher informs me.

"Of course." I grin and am suddenly swept up in Asher's strong arms, held close to his chest, and I hold my arms out for Casey, who happily joins us.

Home.

Home is where they are.

Epilogue

One Year Later
~Asher~

She's in my arms, which is exactly where she belongs, and where I intend to keep her for about the next sixty years. The music is soft and slow. Twinkling lights are in the trees overhead, the ancient oak trees are heavy with Spanish moss, and about fifty of our nearest and dearest are looking on as I dance with my wife for the first time.

"I'm so glad we had the wedding here," Lila murmurs happily. "It was so nice of Kate to hook up with a family that has a gorgeous bed and breakfast in the bayou."

"So nice of her," I agree with a smirk. "You make me laugh."

"I'll make you laugh for a long time," she says sweetly. Her long hair is swept back from her face, and the dress she's in is amazing.

I know that ten years from now I won't remember exactly what it looked like, but I'll remember that she's the most beautiful woman I've ever seen.

"You're a good dancer," she says.

"Those lessons paid off," I reply and roll my eyes. "Why did we do the lessons again?"

"Because it was fun, and so we could dance here like this."

"I don't need lessons to dance with my wife."

Her smile is bright and wide, and makes the breath catch in my lungs.

"You say the sweetest things. Is that going to stop now that I'm the ball and chain?"

I chuckle and kiss her forehead, breathing her in. "You're not the ball and chain."

"Battle-ax?"

"No."

"The old lady?"

"Stop." I kiss her lightly, earning applause from our family and friends. "You're the best part of my life, Delila. From day one, life has been so easy with you. You fell into my lap on that plane, and since that moment, all I could see, all I wanted, was *you*."

"You saved me," she whispers in return. "And I don't mean from Colin."

"I know."

She leans in and lays her cheek on my chest, breaking the hold we learned in class, and we're just swaying back and forth now, under the twinkling lights, in the fresh night air of the bayou, and nothing has ever felt so right in my life.

Sign up for the 1001 Dark Nights Newsletter
and be entered to win a Tiffany Key necklace.

There's a contest every month!

Go to www.1001DarkNights.com to subscribe.

As a bonus, all newsletter subscribers will receive a free
1001 Dark Nights story
The First Night
by Lexi Blake & M.J. Rose

Turn the page for a full list of the
1001 Dark Nights fabulous novellas...

1001 Dark Nights

WICKED WOLF by Carrie Ann Ryan
A Redwood Pack Novella

WHEN IRISH EYES ARE HAUNTING by Heather Graham
A Krewe of Hunters Novella

EASY WITH YOU by Kristen Proby
A With Me In Seattle Novella

MASTER OF FREEDOM by Cherise Sinclair
A Mountain Masters Novella

CARESS OF PLEASURE by Julie Kenner
A Dark Pleasures Novella

ADORED by Lexi Blake
A Masters and Mercenaries Novella

HADES by Larissa Ione
A Demonica Novella

RAVAGED by Elisabeth Naughton
An Eternal Guardians Novella

DREAM OF YOU by Jennifer L. Armentrout
A Wait For You Novella

STRIPPED DOWN by Lorelei James
A Blacktop Cowboys ® Novella

RAGE/KILLIAN by Alexandra Ivy/Laura Wright
Bayou Heat Novellas

DRAGON KING by Donna Grant
A Dark Kings Novella

PURE WICKED by Shayla Black
A Wicked Lovers Novella

HARD AS STEEL by Laura Kaye
A Hard Ink/Raven Riders Crossover

STROKE OF MIDNIGHT by Lara Adrian
A Midnight Breed Novella

ALL HALLOWS EVE by Heather Graham
A Krewe of Hunters Novella

KISS THE FLAME by Christopher Rice
A Desire Exchange Novella

DARING HER LOVE by Melissa Foster
A Bradens Novella

TEASED by Rebecca Zanetti
A Dark Protectors Novella

THE PROMISE OF SURRENDER by Liliana Hart
A MacKenzie Family Novella

FOREVER WICKED by Shayla Black
A Wicked Lovers Novella

CRIMSON TWILIGHT by Heather Graham
A Krewe of Hunters Novella

CAPTURED IN SURRENDER by Liliana Hart
A MacKenzie Family Novella

SILENT BITE: A SCANGUARDS WEDDING by Tina Folsom
A Scanguards Vampire Novella

DUNGEON GAMES by Lexi Blake
A Masters and Mercenaries Novella

AZAGOTH by Larissa Ione
A Demonica Novella

NEED YOU NOW by Lisa Renee Jones
A Shattered Promises Series Prelude

SHOW ME, BABY by Cherise Sinclair
A Masters of the Shadowlands Novella

ROPED IN by Lorelei James
A Blacktop Cowboys ® Novella

TEMPTED BY MIDNIGHT by Lara Adrian
A Midnight Breed Novella

THE FLAME by Christopher Rice
A Desire Exchange Novella

CARESS OF DARKNESS by Julie Kenner
A Dark Pleasures Novella

Also from Evil Eye Concepts:

TAME ME by J. Kenner
A Stark International Novella

THE SURRENDER GATE By Christopher Rice
A Desire Exchange Novel

A BOUQUET FROM M. J. ROSE
A bundle including 6 novels and 1 short story collection

Bundles:

BUNDLE ONE
Includes *Forever Wicked* by Shayla Black
Crimson Twilight by Heather Graham
Captured in Surrender by Liliana Hart
Silent Bite by Tina Folsom

BUNDLE TWO
Includes Dungeon Games by Lexi Blake
Azagoth by Larissa Ione
Need You Now by Lisa Renee Jones
Show My, Baby by Cherise Sinclair

About Kristen Proby

New York Times and USA Today Bestselling Author Kristen Proby is the author of the popular With Me in Seattle series. She has a passion for a good love story and strong characters who love humor and have a strong sense of loyalty and family. Her men are the alpha type—fiercely protective and a bit bossy—and her ladies are fun, strong, and not afraid to stand up for themselves. Kristen spends her days with her muse in the Pacific Northwest. She enjoys coffee, chocolate, and sunshine. And naps. Visit her at KristenProby.com.

Website: http://www.kristenproby.com/
Facebook:
http://www.facebook.com/booksbykristenproby
Twitter: https://twitter.com/Handbagjunkie
Author Goodreads:
http://www.goodreads.com/kristenproby
Novel Goodreads:
https://www.goodreads.com/book/show/23979842-easy-with-you?ac=1

Easy Love
Boudreaux Series, Book 1
By Kristen Proby
Now Available!

Did you enjoy your time in New Orleans? Here is an excerpt from EASY LOVE, book one in the Boudreaux Series, available NOW from all major retailers!

* * * *

My head whips up to stare at Eli. He shoves his hands in his pockets and swears under his breath as he hangs his head then glances back up at me, looking at me like he doesn't really want to be here, and he's not quite sure if he likes me.

"You don't have to stay," I inform him stiffly.

"I don't expect you to work today at all, from here or the office."

"Why ever not?" I lean back in the chair and frown up at him. "You're paying me to work."

"You've traveled all morning, Kate. Settle in. Eat something. In fact, let me take you out to eat something."

"I don't think that's necessary."

"I do." He removes his suit jacket after taking his sunglasses out of the inside pocket and drapes it over the back of the sofa. He rolls the sleeves of the white shirt that molds over his muscled torso all the way up to his elbows, unbuttons the top two buttons, and removes his soft blue tie. "That's better. Go change into something more comfortable, and I'll feed you the best jambalaya you've ever had."

"I've never had jambalaya before," I reply with a raspy voice. I can't tear my eyes off his broad shoulders.

"This will ruin you for all other jambalaya; I promise you."

I frown and meet his gaze, trying to figure him out. "Are

you sure?"

He nods and waits expectantly. I have a feeling not many people say no to Eli Boudreaux.

"I'm not going to sleep with you." The words are out of my mouth before I can reel them back in. I feel my face flame, but I tilt my chin up and square my shoulders firmly.

"I didn't invite you to," he replies calmly, but his eyes are full of humor.

I nod and walk back to the bedroom to change into a light summer dress, slather on sunblock with SPF 4000 to protect my white, freckled skin, and then rejoin Eli, who is now looking out my windows.

"You're always looking out windows," I remark with a smile. He turns to me and his eyes heat as he looks me up and down, and I suddenly feel very exposed.

"You'll burn, *cher*."

"I'm wearing sunblock."

"Do you always argue?" he asks.

"I don't argue."

He holds my gaze for a moment and then tosses his head back and laughs, shakes his head, and leads me out into the hot afternoon.

"Let's go this way first." He turns to the left and rests his hand on the small of my back again, ever the gentleman, walking me down Royal Street. If you'd asked me yesterday if I thought I'd be walking in the French Quarter with the sexiest man I'd ever seen by my side, I would have told you to consult a doctor.

And Eli Boudreaux *is* sexy. But he's not mine, and he never will be. He's my boss, and he's being kind.

I take a deep breath, determined to pull my head out of the gutter and enjoy New Orleans, when Eli pulls me into a trendy shoe and accessory shop called *Head Over Heels*.

"Shoes!" I exclaim, already salivating. Okay, so the man is showing me shoes. I might sleep with him after all.

"Hats," he corrects me.

"Holy crap, what are you doing here?" A woman with short, dark hair and full lips smiles from behind the counter.

"Kate needs a hat," Eli replies and grins as his sister launches herself into his arms and holds on tight.

"Been a minute," she whispers in his ear in the same New Orleans drawl. Eli grins.

"You saw me at Mama's last Sunday."

"Been a minute," she replies and steps back, smiling at me. "Hi, Kate. It's good to see you again."

"You too, Charly." I'm pulled into another hug—the Boudreaux family is an affectionate bunch, and the middle sister, Charlotte, is no different from the rest.

"What can I do for you two?"

"Kate needs a hat," Eli repeats.

"I do?"

"Oh, yes, sugar, you do," Charly replies with a nod. "We need to keep the sun off your face and shoulders. Let's see…" She leads us to the back of the shop and pulls three hats off the wall, all wide-brimmed and pretty. "I think green is your color, with that beautiful auburn hair and your pretty green eyes."

"Thank you, but this hair is about to be a curly tangled mess with all this humidity."

"I know the feeling. I'll make a list of hair products to use while you try these on." She jogs back to her counter as I plop the first hat on my head. It's pink, not quite as widely brimmed as the green, and makes me look like a mushroom.

"Try the green one," Eli suggests, but instead I pull on one with a rainbow of colors. It looks like a box of Crayolas exploded all over it. Eli just watches me in the mirror with humor-filled eyes and crosses his arms over his impressive chest. "You do have beautiful hair."

"Thank you." His jaw ticks. If he doesn't like giving out compliments, why does he say anything at all?

"Oh no, dawlin', the green one," Charly says as she rejoins

us. I smirk as I put the green hat on and sigh as I realize that she and Eli were right.

"Looks like this is the winner," I say with a grin. "I'll take it." I pull my wallet out of my handbag, but Eli lays his hand over mine and shakes his head.

"Bill me," he tells Charly, who smiles and nods happily, while handing me a list of hair products to try, waving at us as Eli leads me back out into the heat. "Feel better?"

"Hmm," I murmur, but, oh, God, yes, it feels so much better. "Thanks for the hat."

"You are welcome," he replies, his accent making me squirm again. I met this man just a few hours ago, and so far, everything he does makes me squirm.

Not good. Not good at all.

"Tell me about yourself," I say, surprising myself. All I know is, I need to get my brain on something other than the mass of testosterone walking next to me. We cross the street, me on the outside, and Eli immediately trades places with me, tucking me next to him away from the street. "Chivalry isn't dead," I whisper.

"No, dawlin', it's not." He flashes me a quick smile before leading me to a café with beautiful courtyard seating.

"It's surprisingly cool in here," I murmur after we're seated.

"The trees keep it cool," the waitress says with a smile. "Need a minute with the menu?"

"Do you eat seafood?" Eli asks me.

"Yes," I reply.

"Good. We'll both have the seafood jambalaya, please."

The waitress nods and walks away, leaving us alone.

"Now, tell me more about your plans to catch the person stealing from my company."

"You didn't answer my question first," I reply, and butter a piece of the bread the waitress just set down for us.

"What question?"

"Tell me about you."

"I don't matter." His voice is calm, but sure. Final. He leans back, folds his arms, and shutters immediately close over his eyes.

Interesting.

"It's your company, so yes, I do believe you matter."

"All you need to know about me is that I'm your boss, you'll be paid timely, and I expect nothing but your best on this job."

I set my bread on a small white plate and lean back, mirroring his pose with my arms crossed. "Actually, I believe it was Savannah who hired me, and I don't ever give less than my best. Ever."

He raises a brow and cocks his head to the side. "Beau, Savannah, and I hold equal shares and equal interest in the company. All three of us are your bosses, Kate."

"Understood." He watches me for several minutes. I can't figure him out. He has moments of being so kind, *nice*, and I think he may be attracted to me, and then the walls come slamming down and he's distant, impersonal, and borderline rude.

Which is it?

On behalf of 1001 Dark Nights,
Liz Berry and M.J. Rose would like to thank ~

Steve Berry
Doug Scofield
Kim Guidroz
Jillian Stein
Dan Slater
Asha Hossain
Chris Graham
Pamela Jamison
Jessica Johns
Richard Blake
BookTrib After Dark
InkSlinger PR
and Simon Lipskar